MONDAY'S CHILD

By

Georgeanne Hayes

Erotic Historical Romance

New Concepts   Georgia

Be sure to check out our website for the very best in fiction at fantastic prices!

When you visit our webpage, you can:

* Read excerpts of currently available books
* View cover art of upcoming books and current releases
* Find out more about the talented artists who capture the magic of the writer's imagination on the covers
* Order books from our backlist
* Find out the latest NCP and author news--including any upcoming book signings by your favorite NCP author
* Read author bios and reviews of our books
* Get NCP submission guidelines
* And so much more!

We offer a 20% discount on all new Trade Paperback releases ordered from our website!

Be sure to visit our webpage to find the best deals in e-books and paperbacks! To find out about our new releases as soon as they are available, please be sure to sign up for our newsletter (http://www.newconceptspublishing.com/newsletter.htm) or join our reader group (http://groups.yahoo.com/group/new_concepts_pub/join)!

The newsletter is available by double opt in only and our customer information is *never* shared!

Visit our webpage at:
www.newconceptspublishing.com

New Concepts Publishing
5202 Humphreys Rd.
Lake Park, GA 31636

ISBN 1-58608-727-4
© copyright Georgeanne Hayes

Cover art (c) copyright Jenny Dixon

NCP books are available at special quantity discounts for bulk purchases for sales promotions, premiums, fund raising, or educational use. For details, write, email, or phone New Concepts Publishing, 5202 Humphreys Rd., Lake Park, GA 31636; Ph. 229-257-0367, Fax 229-219-1097; orders@newconceptspublishing.com.

First NCP Paperback Printing: 2005

Monday's child is fair of face....
England 1818

Chapter One

Moreland Abbey's ancient walls had not seen such a gathering in over a hundred years. Demitria Standish knew that because she knew the Abbey's history far better than any living Moreland. Glancing around at the knots of people gathered in her Aunt Alma's hall as she moved among the guests as unremarked as a wraith, Demi decided to qualify that thought. Correctly speaking, the place had *never* known anything quite like the gathering this evening.

The ladies were dressed in the elegant, stylish draperies of the Empire style. Quite modestly, too, since there were none of London's more daring ladies attendant with their scandalously thin, and sometimes even dampened skirts, and even more scandalous necklines.

The gentlemen were another matter.

They had a notable Corinthian among them, none other than Garrett Trowbridge, Viscount Wyndham. Typically, he was dressed with subdued elegance in almost unrelieved black. Though she'd stolen several surreptitious peeks at him as she wandered restlessly about the huge room that had in ancient times been known as the great hall, Demi hadn't actually had to see him to know that. He had attached himself to her cousin Phoebe's growing circle of admirers some weeks before illness had forced them to abandon the season and hastily depart London, and had long since become a familiar sight to her.

Those men present who cherished the thought of considering themselves in the good company of so notable a sportsman were dressed in a like manner, though not nearly as elegant since few could rival the handsome viscount in face or form.

However, there were a number of dandies in attendance and their attire was not nearly so subdued. They favored more colorful attire and sported stripped or floral waistcoats topped by coats of charcoal or navy. And even the dandies were vastly overshadowed by the macaronis.

Those strutted among the ladies' whites and pastels, the Corinthian's somber blacks, and the conservative blues, grays and purples of the dandy, sporting all the brightest hues of the rainbow. They favored the very extreme of fashion with their wasp waists, exaggeratedly padded shoulders, enormous buckles and buttons and wore heels so high they minced when they walked. Their waistcoats were gorgeous indeed; broadly stripped in bars of scarlet and green, or black and white; some boldly embroidered with cabbage roses, butterflies or bees, above breeches that sometimes matched, and sometimes did not, the tightly fitted jackets they wore over their gorgeous waistcoats.

Settling herself finally on the horsehair sofa at a little distance from the one occupied by her cousin, Phoebe, and Phoebe's admiring court, Demi studied these last with a mixture of amused contempt and purest curiosity. Just as it was inconceivable to her that Phoebe encouraged this set to dangle after her, it was impossible for her to fathom why the macaronis would wish to dress themselves as figures of fun only to attract attention. She didn't care to be the object of curious interest herself, and certainly would not wish it under those circumstances.

She was happy enough to observe and be ignored, which was just as well since she generally was. In truth, she didn't even particularly wish to observe, having seen sufficient social functions in London to appease her curiosity about them, and would have simply remained in her room if not for the fact that she knew her Aunt Alma would notice her absence and remark upon it with disapproval once the guests had taken their leave.

And no one displeased Aunt Alma with impunity.

After a moment, she dismissed the macaronis, for in truth she had little interest in studying their ridiculous dress or observing their affected mannerisms.

She had a great deal of interest in observing Garrett Trowbridge, which was why she'd chosen the position she had, at no great distance from him, where her view was almost completely unobstructed. Nerving herself, feeling as breathless and light headed as if she were contemplating a leap from the barn loft into a haystack, Demi allowed her gaze to skim lightly over him as if she were merely glancing around the room.

She was not surprised to discover Phoebe held his entire attention, nor was she perturbed. Instead, some of her uneasiness dissipated and a tentative surge of enjoyment filled her.

She supposed there were more handsome men in England, but she had yet to see one who appealed to her more. He was tall, of medium build and as classically handsome as any of the men depicted in the Elgin marbles. Despite his dark hair and dark blue eyes, she would have been tempted to think of him as angelically fair if not for the mischievous amusement that so often glinted in his eyes. That was a dead give away that he was anything but angelic even before she'd learned that he was considered a very wild young man in his first years on the town and had scarcely settled a whit in the years since.

Regardless, Aunt Alma had been avidly anticipating receiving him as a son-in-law ever since he'd first cast his interest in Phoebe's direction. Phoebe, herself, waited in breathless anticipation for him to pop the question as well, though Demi was inclined to think that Phoebe was not so enamored with his person as she was with his wealth and title.

As if sensing her gaze, Garrett looked up at that moment and Demi looked down at her hands in her lap, frowning faintly at her thoughts. In the next moment, one of the macaronis spoke to Phoebe and Demi tensed, glad that fate had given her the chance to guard her expression.

"I say, that companion of yours is a queer bird. Is she a mute?" he asked with a titter, glancing toward Demi out of the corner of his eye since his shirt points were so exaggerated he had difficulty turning his head.

The fop beside him, his bosom companion, snickered. "You can't mean to compare her to a swan? It would be an offense to the poor bird," he commented in a tone that was perfectly audible to everyone in the group, and to Demi, as well, despite his pretense of voicing his witticism sotto voce.

Phoebe Moreland tried to look both shocked and offended. It took no great intelligence, though, to see that she was not-so-secretly amused, as well, and trying very hard not to be pleased over the fact that her admirers considered her cousin so unfavorably. "For shame, Mr. Randall! And you, too, Mr. Henson! That's monstrous cruel and I'll not have it! Demi Standish is my cousin, I'll have you to know!"

She glanced toward Demi, adjusting her expression to a nicety to one of both compassion and protectiveness. "Of course she can speak! It's only that she has a..uh..a bit of a lisp and she's uncomfortable talking to anyone she doesn't know well."

Garrett Trowbridge fixed Phoebe with an unfathomable look that nevertheless made her squirm. At nine and twenty, he was the eldest and most dashing of her court of admirers. Wealthy, titled, and blessed with a face and form that had made many a damsel before her cast hopeful, covetous eyes in his direction, his advent into Phoebe's circle had been quite a feather in her cap as far as her fond parent was concerned. For herself, Phoebe wasn't certain whether she was more flattered or disconcerted by his interest since she, unfortunately, had the uncomfortable suspicion that he was also the least enthralled.

Of a certainty, he was the least to be depended upon. She had been convinced when he appeared in the countryside hard upon the heels of her rustication, that he meant to press his suit. Instead, like a willo'wisp, he was there and gone again, attending almost every function she attended for a time and then disappearing for days or weeks on end before he reappeared once more.

An expression of amusement settled upon his

handsome features as he very pointedly and measuringly studied each member of the group before finally his gaze came to rest upon the two macaronis, decked out in all their most beautiful finery. "I sincerely trust you don't mean to liken us all to fowl, Henson. While I suppose it's true the assemblage here might be rather unflatteringly compared to a gaggle of geese, pouter pigeons, clucking hens, or...." He paused significantly as he surveyed the macaroni's attire from the tip of his pointed shoes to the elaborate wig upon his head. "...Strutting peacocks, I'm sure they wouldn't care to have it pointed out to them and I well know I wouldn't."

Henson tittered nervously. "Well! Upon my word, Trowbridge! There's no need to take me up! It was merely an observation."

"And an impertinence," Trowbridge responded lazily.

Phoebe frowned, casting an accusing glance in her cousin's direction, as if Demi, by her mere presence, was entirely responsible for the uncomfortable situation. "I do hope you don't mean to be unpleasant to poor Mr. Henson, my lord."

Garrett's dark brows lifted in a mild expression of surprise, as if he, who was quite notorious for dueling at the drop of a hat, couldn't imagine that she was suggesting he would provoke a fight. In fairness, he'd rarely been known to, for he was in general a very agreeable fellow. However, he was not so amiable that he ignored blatant insults, nor was he at all loathe to accept whatever challenges fell his way. "On no account, my dear! I was merely, as Henson before me, making an observation. However, as I can see I've distressed you, I'll tender my apologies and withdraw."

With that remark and a smile that encompassed the group, he rose and sauntered away.

For once Demi was scarcely aware of his departure. She was concentrating fiercely upon pretending to be deaf and completely unaware of the remarks she'd overheard. Aunt Alma's remarks about eavesdroppers echoed in the back of her mind, but then she hadn't been eavesdropping. They had known she was there, had almost certainly known she would overhear. It could have been nothing but deliberate. The thing was, she couldn't understand why.

Phoebe's behavior, she understood well enough. Phoebe was fond of her in her own way. However, it had been plain from the time Demi had first come to live with the Morelands after her parents' deaths that she was considered an interloper. Phoebe had resented Demi's inclusion in 'her' family from the very first.

It hurt nonetheless.

Henson and Randall's assault were incomprehensible. She'd never, to her knowledge, done anything to warrant such an attack. She frowned, wondering if perhaps she had not concealed her contempt of their affections as well as she'd thought. Or maybe it hadn't even needed that? Possibly it was sufficient that she had shown no admiration?

That thought dulled the prick of hurt and she dismissed it as something too insignificant to allow it to wound. She didn't care for their opinion, after all.

She did, however, care about Garrett Trowbrige's opinion. She would far rather he had not heard that exchange between Phoebe and her beaus.

It wasn't that she considered it at all likely that Garrett would notice her in a favorable way. She was not nearly beautiful enough or wealthy enough for that, particularly when she fell under Phoebe's shadow. But it would be far better to be ignored than to be looked upon with pity or contempt.

She wished suddenly that she had not yielded to the temptation to see Garrett and the apprehension of provoking her Aunt's wrath and joined the guests. She wished she could simply vanish from their midst.

Unfortunately, she couldn't. Nor would she contemplate for more than a moment retreating like a scalded cat under the barrage of their insults. She had her pride, if she had little else.

Therefore, she remained where she was, doing her best to appear completely at ease, when she wasn't, and totally unconcerned with what anyone thought of her. She had decided some time later that she had lingered in her aunt's salon long enough to save face and had risen to leave when a slight commotion at the door caught her attention. Vaguely curious of the identity of the late arrivals, Demi turned to look and felt an odd mixture of dismay and delight when she saw that the couple that had arrived was Pastor Flemming and his daughter Esmeralda.

The pleasure was reserved entirely for Esme, who had long been her best friend. Her dread derived from the fact that Esme's father, a widower of thirty and eight, had apparently been laboring under the mistaken belief for the past several months that Demi welcomed him as a suitor.

Jonathan Flemming was not unhandsome, but then neither were his harshly angular features particularly appealing to Demi, though it seemed she was a majority of one. Most of the women of the parish apparently considered him exceptionally attractive if the number of widows who'd courted him over the years since his wife had died in childbirth was any indication.

It was not that alone, however, that lacked appeal. Nor was Demi particularly put off by the number of years that separated them, for he was by no means stricken with age. Rather, it was his size she found discomfiting.

Though it was certainly a source of constant awe, the fact that he stood head and shoulders above most men made her feel over powered and distinctly uneasy when he was in her proximity. Moreover, contrary to the myth of gentle giants, Jonathan Flemming seemed as harsh and unyielding as his features implied. He had little patience for fools or sinners and no discernible sense of humor. She was torn on the instant with an equal desire both to take flight at once and disappear as quickly and unobtrusively as possible, and the conviction that she owed it to Esme, who was as uncomfortable at these functions as she was herself, to stay and bear her friend company. She never actually arrived at a decision.

Alma Moreland, her aunt, had no sooner welcomed the late arrivals that she turned and fixed Demi with a look that was both a summons and a warning. Jonathan Flemming followed the direction of her aunt's gaze and pinned Demi with a proprietary smile. Esme's expression was both nervous and apologetic as her father promptly excused himself to Alma Morcland and made his way toward Demi.

Dismayed, Demi glanced around, seeking an avenue of escape, knowing even as she did so that she was fairly caught now and could not do so without being unforgivably rude. Still, her gaze touched longingly upon the door nearest her and it occurred to her that escape was near enough that, should Jonathan Flemming be distracted only for a few moments, she could and would seize her chance.

No such distraction occurred, unfortunately. She'd scarcely glanced around when Flemming was addressing her. "Ah! Miss Standish! I see you're in your usual looks tonight, my dear!"

Reluctantly, Demi turned to face him. As she did so her gaze clashed with that of Garrett Trowbridge, who was propped against the wall quite near the door Demi had been eyeing with such longing.

Either he had rejoined Phoebe's group or, more likely, Phoebe had thought of an excuse to encompass him in her circle once more. Phoebe's group was now clustered between the refreshment table and the door that led to the kitchens, virtually surrounding Garrett, despite the fact that he bore all the appearance of being totally detached from their conversation and was, instead, gazing out across the room.

With some difficulty, Demi focused her attention upon Flemming. Pasting a civil smile of welcome upon her lips, she responded with the expected reply, firmly tamping the temptation to utter one of the remarks her aunt considered outrageous and was forever scolding her for.

"Thank you," she murmured, and then, glancing down at her gown uncomfortably, succumbed to temptation after all. "At least, I suppose you meant that as a compliment?"

She was wearing a cast off of her cousin, and though she'd long since ceased to be extremely self-conscious about wearing Phoebe's hand-me-downs, it did nothing for her confidence to appear at her aunt's grand social functions in gowns that had previously been seen everywhere upon Phoebe. The gown she wore tonight was as well, if not better, than any other in her wardrobe. However, while it had complimented Phoebe's fair perfection, it did not flatter Demi's chestnut locks and hazel eyes nearly so well. Moreover, although far from tatters, it was also very evident that the gown had seen a good deal of wear. Where once it had been the color of bluebells, it was now an indeterminate shade that was neither blue nor gray. If that were not evidence enough that the gown had seen better days, the fit certainly suggested as much.

At five feet six inches, Demi was several inches taller than her cousin. She was also, regrettably for the sake of modesty, a good bit more endowed in her bosom. As a result, the gown bore unmistakable signs of being 'outgrown' both in length and fit. It was not only too short, but her bosom looked as if it might burst the seams of the bodice at any moment, a state that Demi had tried her best to disguise by tossing a light wrap around her shoulders. The end result of that effort was that she looked entirely dowdy. Unfortunately, she knew it.

Flemming frowned disapprovingly, but then patted her arm. "Certainly it was a compliment, my dear. Surely you didn't think otherwise?"

Demi smiled at him a little doubtfully and turned her attention to Esme, smiling this time with genuine warmth. "Hello, Esme," she said and hugged her friend impulsively. "Don't you look pretty tonight! When did you get back? I missed you something fierce! Did you enjoy your stay with your cousins?"

Esme smiled gratefully and smoothed the skirts of her gown self-consciously.

Poor Esme was as squat as her father was tall, and nearly as big around as she was high. Cursed with her father's features, if not his stature, that same face in feminine form was not softened to beauty or even to prettiness. Rather, Esme was almost painfully plain. She might have benefited had she also inherited her father's dark, glossy locks. Instead, contrary nature had given her hair that was a mousy, uncertain shade somewhere between blond and brown.

She had been blessed, however, with a quick wit and a

personality that was almost pure beauty.

Chuckling at Demi's barrage, she said, "I've only just come back today or I would've been over to see you, you must know."

Jon Flemming chuckled as well, though the sound was somewhat strained. "Nothing would do her but to come tonight, though I know well she's bound to be fagged from the trip."

Esme sent her father a look, but didn't dispute him. She didn't need to in any event. Even if not for that telltale glance of surprise, Demi knew Esme well enough to have seen the remark for the whopper it was. Esme, to her father's irritation, was 'bookish' and cared for socializing even less than Demi, if possible.

Jon Flemming had his own reasons for coming tonight and Demi very much feared she knew what that reason was. Almost as if on cue with that thought the musicians her aunt had hired took up their instruments and struck up the first notes of a dance. Demi's heart sank as Flemming smiled and reached for her hand. "May I have this dance?" he asked.

She didn't know why he bothered to voice the statement as a request, for it was certainly not that. His attitude and tone were plainly proprietary.

Before Demi could think up an excuse to reject him, someone touched her elbow. She glanced around quickly to discover Garrett Trowbridge had come to stand beside her and felt the earth drop from beneath her feet as she gazed up into his dazzlingly brilliant grin. "Our dance, I believe. Better luck next time, Flemming. She's already promised this dance to me."

The shock alone should have been sufficient to prevent Demi from behaving in any way approaching normal. In truth, she was not afterwards certain how her behavior might have appeared to anyone who happened to observe it, but the need to escape overrode all other considerations. She had murmured her apologies and placed her hand on Lord Wyndham's sleeve and departed with him for the dance floor before she thought better of it.

Unfortunately, she began to wonder almost immediately why he'd seen fit to rescue her. A half a dozen possibilities came almost instantly to mind, none of them particularly flattering to her, but, when all was said and done, did it really matter what his motives were? "Thank you," she said quietly.

His dark brows rose. "You are premature. We have not danced yet and you may feel less inclined to thank me once we have."

Demi glanced at him in surprise and bit back a smile. "For rescuing me," she clarified, although she doubted he'd misunderstood her to begin with.

"You're so certain that was my motivation?" he asked pensively.

"It wasn't?" Demi asked in surprise. "Well, I won't ask, for I'm ever so grateful you did, whatever your reasons."

"A burning desire to engage in a country dance?"

She chuckled. "I could believe most anything but that."

"As it happens, I haven't been called upon to rescue a demoiselle in distress in quite some time. I found it difficult to resist the desperate glance you cast in my direction."

"Oh, but I didn't--" Demi broke off. Blushing, she bit her lip, realizing that the comment she'd been about to make could easily be considered rude. On the other hand, it was almost as embarrassing to think that he'd been laboring under the assumption that she'd cast a beseeching plea in his direction. It wouldn't have occurred to her to look to him to come to her rescue, for she'd barely even exchanged pleasantries with him previously.

His dark brows rose. "You didn't?" he prompted.

Demi looked at him uncomfortably. "I only glanced at the door. I was wondering if I was close enough...."

A faint smile curled his lips. "I am properly set down."

"I beg your pardon. That was rude, but I didn't mean to be."

He didn't look put out. In fact, he looked at her for the first time with an air of keen interest. "But refreshingly honest, nevertheless."

Demi cast a quick glance around the room. "Aunt Alma would not be at all pleased to think she has not cured me of my 'refreshing honesty' when she has been at such pains to teach me how to behave in polite society."

Fortunately, they reached the dance floor at that moment and were obliged to take up their positions for the country dance, precluding further speech, for Demi had no sooner made the remark than it occurred to her that that opened the door to questions she'd as soon not answer. Unfortunately, her aunt caught her eye at just that moment and, even from across a crowded room, her look of promised retribution was such that Demi found it difficult to concentrate on the dance. In the end, not only did she perform with embarrassing clumsiness, but she did not enjoy a dance that should have become a momentous memory for her--her first, and quite possibly only, dance with the man she had secretly adored from afar from the first moment she'd set eyes upon him.

Chapter Two

Retribution was swift in coming. Demitria had spent far more of her life with her aunt than she had with the parents she could scarcely remember, and knew well enough to expect that it would. Nevertheless, the sheer magnitude of her aunt's revenge succeeded in stunning her.

She'd been obliged to remain at the soiree once her dance with Lord Wyndham had been concluded despite her near desperation by that time to escape, for her aunt kept her under her watchful eye for the remainder of the evening. Nor could she think of an acceptable excuse to refuse Jon Flemming's invitation to dance afterward. In the end, she had been obliged to dance twice with him and it was only for the sake of propriety that he accepted her refusal of a third.

By the time she'd been allowed to retire, she'd had a headache from parrying Flemming's determined flirtation the remainder of the evening. She awoke the following day with her head still pounding and was greeted by her maid with the intelligence that her aunt wanted a word with her directly after she'd broken her fast.

It was enough to demolish what little appetite she'd had. The rare streak of rebellion-- courtesy, according to her aunt, of her father--that her aunt had not succeeded in completely eliminating had reared its head, however, and instead of presenting herself immediately, she went for a stroll in the garden in the hope that it might lift her spirits, or at least reduce her pounding headache.

It didn't, and after a time, she wandered into the meadow of tall grasses beyond the garden. Darting a quick look around to make certain she was not observed, she sat, staring up at the sky dreamily, trying to summon the dim memories of her childhood to bring her some measure of peace. She remembered happiness, but only tiny snatches of particular events. Her father, a soldier, had been stationed in India and she and her mother had gone to live with him there. She knew she'd been there when her parents were killed in the uprising, but oddly enough, she couldn't recall any of it. The doctor had said that the images were simply too horrendous for her to accept and so her mind had shielded her from the memory. She suspected that he was correct in his assumption and therefore had never tried to find those lost memories. She supposed that was why she remembered so little of the good memories either, but those she deeply regretted losing.

She wasn't certain of whether she dozed, or if she slipped so deeply into her thoughts that she lost awareness of her surroundings. Whichever the case, her mind was slow to interpret the thrashing in the nearby grass as footsteps and he was virtually upon her before it connected in her mind. She sat up with a start, her heart beating unpleasantly fast. She didn't know whether to be relieved or further disturbed when she discovered that it was Lord Wyndham. Even looking upon him was enough to make her almost giddily breathless with excitement, but his attention unnerved her almost as much as it thrilled her.

"I have found our truant, I believe."

She looked up at him guiltily. "My lord?"

"The picnic?" he prompted.

Demi put a hand to her wildly fluttering heart. "I thought perhaps my aunt was looking for me," she said with a touch of relief. She'd forgotten her cousin had planned a picnic for the day, but then she had not been invited and she had not really paid much attention to the plans Phoebe and her court were making for their entertainment.

Amusement gleamed in his eyes. He looked the grass over with a touch of doubt and finally settled on the ground facing her, wrapping his arms around his bent knees. "So … you *are* playing truant."

Demi sighed but finally nodded. "It's far too early in the day to face unpleasantness, especially when one has a headache to begin with."

"Most ladies physic headaches by lying in a darkened

room with a tistane," he said pensively, "not a meadow beneath the sun."

Grimacing, Demi looked away. "I expect, then, that they do not have an aunt like mine."

"She strikes me as a veritable dragon."

Demi looked at him sharply and looked away again, plucking a blade of grass and twining it about her fingers. "I expect I sound ungrateful for all my aunt has done for me. Truly, I'm not. She has been most generous in caring for me, considering I've not a farthing to my name."

"Mmm," he murmured non-committally. "And what plans has this generous aunt of yours devised for your future, I wonder? I expect Lady Phoebe will be settled before the year is out and will no longer have need of a companion."

In point of fact, although her aunt had not elaborated on her thoughts, she had expressed the opinion that it would be cheaper in the long run to settle a modest dowry upon Demi than to have her niece swung about her neck for the remainder of her life. Demi correctly interpreted modest to mean a sum sufficient to attract a tradesman or perhaps a man with a profession. Her aunt was beyond tight with a farthing. She had suffered over launching Phoebe in style, but had explained that she expected the expense to prove well worth it, for Phoebe was bound to land a man of wealth and title.

Instead of answering, she rose abruptly and brushed the grass and dirt from her frock. As uncomfortable as the conversation itself was, she shuddered to think what her aunt might have to say about her speaking with Lord Wyndham. "Excuse me. I should go in now. It is never wise to keep Aunt Alma waiting overlong."

She cast a look behind her when she reached the garden once more, wondering if it was possible that she might have been observed from the house. To her dismay, she could see Lord Wyndham quite clearly.

She doubted her cousin would suffer any anxiety over Lord Wyndham's sudden, and completely incomprehensible, interest in her, but her aunt would not take it kindly at all and might well accuse her of throwing herself in his way.

Her aunt, she discovered when she inquired of one of the maids, had ensconced herself in her late husband's study. A deep sense of foreboding settled over Demi as she made way down the hall to the door of the study and tapped lightly. She was given permission to enter and, taking a deep, sustaining breath, went in.

"Did your maid not give you my message?" Alma Moreland greeted her.

Demi stared at her aunt. If she said no, then the maid would either be dismissed or severely reprimanded. If she said yes, she would have to endure the barrage herself. As tempted as she was to deny responsibility, however, she was fond of her maid and didn't want to get her into trouble. "Yes, Aunt Alma ... but I had a headache and went out in the hopes that fresh air would help."

Her aunt gave her a look that left her in no doubt that she knew Lord Wyndham had joined her. "With whom?"

Blushing beneath that unforgiving stare despite all she could do, Demi furnished her aunt with a half truth. She did not expect to get away with it, for her Aunt Alma was very like a demi-god in that absolutely nothing transpired at Moreland that she was unaware of. Demi strongly suspected that at least half of the servants were her spies and reported to her hourly. "I went to walk in the garden alone."

"Where you encountered Lord Wyndham? Did you make an assignation with him last eve when the two of you danced?"

Demi gaped at her aunt in shock. "No!"

Alma Moreland studied her for several moments and finally nodded. "You will do well to eschew his company in future, my dear. He has a shocking reputation."

Resentment swelled in Demi's breast. It was an outright fabrication, and she knew it. He had sown his share of wild oats ... and what young man of the ton had not? But he was certainly not a blackguard as her aunt seemed to be implying. "I find that difficult to believe!" she exclaimed before she thought better of it.

"Are you questioning my word?" Alma Moreland

asked coldly.

Demi paled and looked down at her hands. She had not been invited to sit and she shifted uncomfortably under her aunt's piercing stare. "Surely you would not allow him to court Phoebe if he was beyond the pale?"

"Quit fidgeting!" Alma Moreland snapped. "As to that, he would not think of giving my girl a slip on the shoulder. You are another matter, my dear. Many an impoverished young woman before you has found herself in dire straights indeed by refusing to listen to the advice of their betters. You will do well to remember that men like Lord Wyndham have their family name to consider. They do not seriously court impoverished young women, even those of good family. They have been known to prey upon them, however, for their baser needs."

Demi didn't know whether to be horrified or intrigued by the suggestion that Lord Wyndham might have dark designs upon her. It had not occurred to her previously that he might. He'd indicated that he'd asked her to dance out of empathy for her reluctance to dance with the Rev. Flemming. She had not thought to question it. As for their encounter earlier, she'd considered it merely a coincidence that he had happened upon her in the meadow.

She frowned, but try as she might she could not think of anything that he'd said or done to indicate he had designs upon her person. Very likely, she decided with some disappointment, it was only her aunt's evil mind that had invented lasciviousness where none existed.

"That said--and I know you are, in general, a modest young woman ," Alma Moreland continued, "I have very good news for you."

Demi's belly clenched reflexively. Good news to Alma Moreland didn't necessarily mean anyone else would think it so. In general it meant that she expected to profit somehow from it, regardless of whom the news pertained to and anyone who did no share her opinion of the news was either a fool or they had set themselves up against her. "Good news?" she echoed cautiously.

"Do sit down, Demitria! From the look of you I can't imagine your stroll was particularly efficacious. You're as pale as a ghost."

Demi looked around and finally perched on the edge of the nearest chair, waiting expectantly for the ax to fall.

Alma Moreland smiled at her and if possible, Demi's stomach clenched even harder. "Our dear Reverend Flemming had a word with me last evening before he left. Such a gentleman! And such a fine figure of a man. He is considered quite a catch, you must know. You have played your cards very well, very well indeed-- although I must say I'm not particularly fond of that vulgarism--But it never does to allow a man to feel as if he has an open field. It was very clever of you to finagle a dance out of Lord Wyndham--just the impetus needed to push Mr. Flemming into declaring himself. We have all but settled it between us. I must say I was most pleasantly surprised by him, for he readily agreed with the sum I offered to settle upon you. In fact, he made it clear that he had not expected that you would be dowered at all and had set aside a sum himself for that purpose." She stopped, frowning. "I was *that* put out about it, I must tell you, for I might have saved ... but no matter. I shall not count the cost in seeing you properly settled. It's the least I can do for my poor, departed sister to see her girl comfortably settled."

If her aunt had announced that she was to be executed the following morning, Demi did not think she could have been more stunned. Bereft of speech, her thoughts shattered into chaos by shock, Demi found she was incapable for some moments of even putting two thoughts together and making any sense of them. At first she could not think beyond her revulsion at the idea of being Jonathan Flemming's wife. Outrage began to sink in as she managed to add to that the fact that he and her aunt between them had settled all very neatly without any consideration for her wishes, without consulting her, without even apprising her of their plans until after the fact.

Alma Moreland smirked. "I see I have rendered you speechless with delight. I confess I was not at all pleased to see you dangling after Lord Wyndham, particularly since I could only consider it a betrayal of trust when you know very well he is Phoebe's beau and we expect almost daily that he will declare himself. Now that I have been brought to see that it was merely a clever ruse on your part to coax the elusive Mr. Flemming into taking the plunge, I am only sorry I did not think of it myself. Men are such territorial creatures when all is said and done, and it is only human nature to want what is difficult to obtain and despise what is easily gotten.

"I must confess I'm a bit put out to see you settled before my own, dear daughter, especially when she is nigh a year your senior, but I did not feel it wise to play fast and loose with your future, my dear, by putting him off until after Phoebe's engagement had been announced."

Demi looked at her aunt blankly. "Phoebe is engaged?"

Alma Moreland reddened. "Sarcasm is most unbecoming in young people, particularly when directed at their elders. You know very well she is not-- not yet, at any rate. I expect she will be soon. In point of fact, it occurs to me that it may take no more than the announcement of your engagement to Mr. Flemming to inspire others to capitulate.

"But, enough of that. I know you are on pins and needles to hear the particulars of your own match. I assured Mr. Flemming that you would welcome his offer and invited him to luncheon today so that he may be private with you afterward while the young people are all off enjoying their picnic."

"But … I do *not* welcome his offer!" Demi blurted out suddenly.

Alma Moreland looked at her in stunned amazement. "I beg your pardon?" she demanded coldly.

A wave of fear washed through Demi, but she was far more fearful of finding herself wed, and completely at the mercy of Jonathan Flemming. If there had been any doubt in her mind that he was of the same ilk as her aunt, she might have been willing to consider it, but she was certain he was every bit as controlling and demanding as her aunt, possibly even more so. Of a certainty, he could also be kind, but that was only when everything was going as he pleased. At any time he was displeased, he was enraged. He hid it reasonably well-- now. Once she was under his control he would have no concern about giving vent to it, she was certain, and his size alone was unnerving. He was built far more like a blacksmith than a cleric. "As much as I appreciate his offer, I can not accept it," Demi stammered.

Alma Moreland's eyes narrowed. "You have options I am unaware of? A dozen beaux waiting in the wings to snap you up? A dowry? Or, perhaps you were thinking more along the lines of entering service? In which case you must have references I am not aware of. Talent that might qualify you to instruct young ladies of family? An education that would make you acceptable as a governess perhaps?"

Demi stared at her aunt in dismay, knowing even without her aunt's cutting remarks that she had no options open to her. Her father had been a charming rogue, but neither wise nor frugal. Her mother's portion had been gone, she felt sure, even before her birth. Her father had inherited even less. The youngest son, his father had purchased his colors and shipped him off to India to seek his fortune.

She'd spent the better part of the past year trying to think what she might do to support herself once Phoebe had married, for her aunt had made it clear almost from the first that she was looking forward to discharging her obligations to her sister's child. She had not been able to come up with a solution, unfortunately, and had come up empty of any idea except a vague one that Phoebe would perhaps consider allowing her a place in her own home.

She might have been willing to consider it, but as headstrong as Phoebe was, she was as cowed by her mother as Phoebe and would not directly oppose her if her mother forbid her to do so.

She licked her dried lips. "I had thought, since Phoebe is to be settled soon, that she might find a place for me in her household."

Alma Moreland gave her a look. "Are you mad? You might well consider becoming a servant in your cousin's home, and I make no doubt that dear Phoebe is kind hearted enough to take you on, but I will not have it said that I did not do my best to see my niece comfortably settled in her own home."

"I am quite accustomed to seeing to Phoebe's needs. I shouldn't mind it at all, and certainly no one could doubt your generosity to me or your earnest efforts to keep my best interests to heart," Demi added placatingly.

If possible, Alma Moreland looked even more outraged. "Are you suggesting that you have been used as a mere servant?"

"Certainly not!" Demi disclaimed immediately. "I am glad to help out in any way I can, knowing what you have expended on my behalf ... and cousin Phoebe is very dear to me. I am only saying that I would not mind being a help to Phoebe, for she is certain to marry well and will have a large household."

"Which you would not be qualified in any way to be of help to her!" Alma Moreland reminded her sharply, not appeased in the least by Demi's attempts to placate her. "I will not hear of it! I have given Mr. Flemming my approval, assured him that you would welcome his offer and you will not disappoint me. Is that clear?"

Demi felt ill. She didn't trust herself to speak. Finally, she managed to nod. She was dismissed, but she felt little relief. Rising a little unsteadily, she left the study. To her dismay, Phoebe's party was milling about the hall, on the point of departure. She glanced blindly in their direction when she heard her name called.

"You are not coming with us?" Phoebe asked, for the second time, Demi dimly realized.

She formed her lips into the semblance of a smile with an effort. "Thank you, but no. I have a touch of headache. I believe I will lie down for a bit."

"Oh! You poor thing! You must ask my maid to fix you up. She has a marvelous cure for headache."

Demi nodded and forced another smile, flicking her gaze across the faces turned toward her before turning away. Gripping the banister, she climbed the stairs with an effort, feeling as stiff and uncoordinated as an elderly woman. It wasn't until she had collapsed upon her bed that the images resolved themselves into individual faces. Lord Wyndham had been among them, his gaze piercing although his face had been a mask of polite boredom.

She wondered a little vaguely if she had given herself away. She had smiled and spoke and comported herself, she thought, remarkably well under the circumstances. Phoebe had not seemed to notice she was laboring under any sort of distress. She could not recall a single smirk that indicated any of the others saw anything in her behavior to amuse them.

It was amazing, really, how often a group of people took on the characteristics of a pack of wolves. Individually, they were seldom predatory, but they had only to find themselves surrounded by their peers to bring out the worst in them, the search for weakness in a loner that they might use to rip them to shreds.

She found she was too distressed to think up an alternative to her aunt's ultimatum. She suspected that, even had she not been distressed, nothing would have come to mind. Her aunt's assessment of her situation was all too true. She did not have enough education to seek a post in teaching. She had no talent with either water colors or musical instruments that might make her desirable to families with daughters. Without her aunt's support, she had no references and no connections to secure a place for herself in service. Her lack of a dowry had been sufficient to discourage any interest in her as a matrimonial prospect with the exception of Mr. Flemming. Her aunt had made it clear enough that she would accept Mr. Flemming's proposal or find herself on the street. The prospect of having no where at all to go was only slightly more frightening than that of marrying Jonathan Flemming.

She finally concluded that it *was* worse, however. On the streets, she would be prey to many men of Mr. Flemming's ilk, or worse, not just the one.

It was a great pity she had not been born with the beauty to become a courtesan. She knew she would be a pariah even for thinking such a thing, but it was almost better to contemplate the life of a mistress or courtesan.

Unfortunately, that was out of the question. So, too, was the wild idea of taking to the stage. If she'd been talented enough, her looks might not have mattered. If she had been beautiful enough, a lack of talent wouldn't have been a problem, but she was fairly certain having neither would only land her in the streets.

The immutable truth was that she was completely at her aunt's mercy, and her aunt had none.

By the time the maid came to summon her to the dreaded luncheon, she had calmed somewhat and realized she had no option other than accepting her fate. She felt distinctly ill. She was also angry with her fate, but she knew she could not fight it.

She got up, washed her face, tidied her hair and smoothed her gown. Dragging in a deep, sustaining breath of air, she left the room and went downstairs to face her future.

Chapter Three

Simple obedience, Demitria knew from past experience, was not sufficient. Her aunt would expect her to be pleased, or give the appearance of it. If she sat like a stone throughout the luncheon, pale, uncommunicative, refusing to eat, her aunt would take it in the same way that she would see open defiance. She would be livid and she would leave Demi in no doubt of it once Mr. Flemming took his leave.

She ate slowly, and with extreme care, to keep from choking or being violently ill when her knotted stomach rejected the food she swallowed determinedly. She managed to smile at every mildly witty remark that Mr. Flemming made and even to participate in the conversation beyond a simple yes or no to questions put to her.

Alma Moreland sent her several approving glances during the course of the meal. Instead of being relieved, however, Demi began to think of them as gloating smirks. Slowly, the shock wore off and anger began to simmer beneath the surface of her calm. Presently, it occurred to her with a touch of surprise that she hated her aunt. She hadn't considered it before. If anyone had asked, she would almost certainly have said, dutifully, that she loved her aunt, but the truth was she had never felt any warmer emotion toward the woman.

She had tried. In the beginning, when she had first come to live with the Morelands, she had wanted desperately to win her aunt's affection. She had hungered for the love she had lost when her parents were killed and had been eager to please. In time, she'd come to realize that Alma Moreland simply was not capable of feeling any affection for anyone beyond herself. It was not only she who failed to engender it. So far as she could tell, Alma Moreland had never felt more than a distant sort of fondness for either Lord Moreland or Phoebe. What little she had to give had been reserved for her son, and Demi was more inclined to think that less akin to love than pride.

There had been a time when she was younger when she had pitied her aunt, certain that some terrible thing had happened to her that made her that way and that, deep down, she suffered. Perhaps it was true, but Demi neither pitied nor empathized with her any longer. Whatever might have occurred to make her the cold, unfeeling, tyrant that she was, was not an excuse for her complete disregard for the feelings of others.

Demi entertained herself thorough the latter half of the meal with fanciful revenges, but in the end she was obliged to admit to herself that there was little hope of her ever being in a position of power that would allow her to seek any sort of satisfactory retribution.

She was well and truly under her aunt's thumb and about to be passed off to another thumb that was probably just as merciless.

Her interview with Jonathan Flemming was as uncomfortable as she'd envisioned but, fortunately, even her own personal purgatory had a time limit. Mr. Flemming professed a great regard for her, all the while staring down at her bosom lasciviously, as if she were sitting before him naked. Demi managed to repress a shudder, pasted a smile on her lips and mouthed the same lie. Her aunt returned to the room, professed her delight at the match, allowed Demi to kiss her cheek, and she and Jonathan Flemming sat down to haggle over the fine points of the settlement. They were still ensconced in the parlor, discussing the nuptials, when the party returned from their picnic.

Phoebe uttered a shriek of delight when her mother announced Demi's engagement and flew across the room to congratulate Demi, evidencing every appearance of genuine excitement. Before Demi knew it, she was surrounding by Phoebe and her friends, chattering so rapidly and excitedly they reminded her far more of a gaggle of geese than a half dozen young women. She accepted their excitement and congratulations, wondering if they were truly as happy for her as they appeared to be, simply excited that someone was getting married in general, or, cynically, if they were thrilled because they no longer had to concern themselves that Jonathan Flemming might cast his handkerchief in their direction.

She finally decided that it was more than likely the second of the two possibilities. They were Phoebe's friends, not hers. If they had been her friends, they would have been commiserating with her, not congratulating her, or possibly the last of the three conjectures. They were none of them in any danger of Mr. Flemming's attentions, though. He was of good family, and apparently well enough off, but he was obviously also aware that he was not considered a great prize on the marriage mart and Phoebe and her friends were above his touch.

The men who'd accompanied the party promptly scattered at the announcement, like a flock of birds startled by the huntsman's gun, disappearing almost before anyone was aware of their intentions. The moment Phoebe and her friends ebbed away, gathering in an excited little knot to pry the particulars from Alma Moreland and Mr. Flemming, Demi rose and headed toward the door.

She'd almost made good her escape when Phoebe stopped her. "You are not leaving when we are right in the middle of planning the wedding?"

Demi smiled wanly. "I feel certain that I can leave it in Aunt Alma and Mr. Flemming's capable hands."

Alma Moreland sent her a narrow eyed glare, but for once Demi found she simply didn't care. Jonathan Flemming was another matter. She didn't particularly like the look he sent her and forced another smile. "In any case, I don't feel at all well and see no reason to expose everyone if I should be coming down with something."

As she'd hoped, that comment was sufficient to quiet even Mr. Flemming's objections to her departure. She left amid instructions, well wishes, and suggestions, moving down the hallway toward the stairs. She'd already reached the foot of the stairs when it dawned upon her that her aunt would almost certainly be up to check on her before very long, to ascertain whether she'd lied or not.

Changing directions, she made her way through the study and out onto the verandah that ran nearly the width of the manor in back. The sun was dipping near the tops of the distant trees and already the air was cool. She shivered, chaffing her arms and wishing she'd thought to grab a shawl. As tempting as the thought was of returning for one, she dismissed it. She'd escaped and she wasn't about to be caught merely because she couldn't bear a little discomfort.

A faint whiff of something burning tickled at her nostrils and she looked around to discover its source. Lord Wyndham was lounging against the wall near the balustrade that ran round the verandah, smoking a cheroot. Nodding, she hurried down the steps and crossed the garden, walking as briskly as her skirts allowed, ladylike be damned.

She had no destination in mind, but as she reached the edge of the garden, she gathered her skirts in her hands and, lifting them out of her way, darted across the meadow. She had not run in years, not since she was a little girl and certainly not since she'd begun to wear a corset. She discovered very quickly that the skirts were not the only impediment to putting as much distance as possible between her and Moreland Abbey. She had not run far when she was forced to stop. Struggling to catch her breath, she dropped to a walk once more, but a wave of nausea washed over her. She came to a complete halt then, struggled to will it away and finally lost the battle and dropped to her knees.

She'd no more than finished being violently ill when someone offered her a handkerchief. She didn't even glance up. "Go away!"

"No. You are ill."

Demi squeezed her eyes closed when she recognized his voice. It needed only that in a very long day of trials. She would not have cared if Jonathan Flemming had stood by while she wretched, in fact the more she repelled him the better she liked the thought. But the stunningly gorgeous and perfect Lord Wyndham? The object of her secret devotion? Was she to have *no* memories even to look back upon with fondness? She took the handkerchief he offered almost angrily and wiped her face and mouth. "I'm fine now. Thank you! Please go away."

Instead of answering or retreating, he grasped her arm and hauled her to her feet. To her surprise, instead of turning toward the house, he glanced around and headed toward the nearest tree. Demi followed him numbly, wishing the ground would open up and swallow her, but even that solace was denied her. They reached the tree without incident. Once there, he shrugged out of his coat, draped it around her shoulders and urged her to sit.

She sat, huddling in his coat, absorbing the warmth that remained from his body, and the wonderful scents that adhered to it. She'd never been particularly fond of the smell of tobacco, or horses, and yet, mingled with the other scents that were his alone, she found it made her feel comforted and edgy at the same time, and strangely warm all over. It occurred to her that she would most likely forever afterward think of him whenever she smelled that particular blend of tobacco.

…Which would be marred by the additional memory of having spilled her lunch in the grass first. She dropped her face into her hands, wondering what she had done to deserve having such horrid things happen to her.

"You're certain you're not coming down with something?" he asked, settling beside her.

"I could not be so fortunate," she muttered morosely.

He chuckled. She felt him digging in the pockets of the coat he'd thrown over her shoulders. She was beginning to wonder what he was about when he pulled a small flask from one pocket, removed the lid and nudged her shoulder. The pungent aroma of strong spirits wafted past her nose. She looked down at the flask, knowing very well she had no business even considering taking a sip of the vile mess, which he most certainly knew as well.

She took the flask, held her breath and took a large sip. It burned her mouth, her throat and finally her stomach as it hit bottom. It snatched the breath out of her lungs so that she sat gasping for several moments. It also scoured the taste of sickness from her mouth, however, and as the burning slowly cooled, warmth seemed to spread outward from the pool of lava in her belly. "Thank you," she managed to say hoarsely after several moments.

Hooking the ball of his fist beneath her chin, he caught her chin with his thumb and forced her to look up at him. Reluctantly, she did. "I had pegged you for a fighter."

She gave him an indignant look and lifted her chin away from his hold.

Shrugging, he capped the flask and dropped it into the pocket of his coat once more. "I couldn't help but notice that you didn't seem particularly pleased about your engagement."

She blushed, but she didn't want pity, and she had no desire to become grist for the local gossip mills--not that she could imagine Lord Wyndham taking part in such a thing, but all the same it would not do to openly oppose the match. Mr. Flemming might be angered enough to withdraw his offer, and the lord only knew what her aunt would do in that event. "It is only that it came as a great surprise. I have not had time to accustom myself to the idea," she said stiffly.

He looked her over with a critical eye, or so it seemed to Demi. "I confess, I find it hard to imagine you was a minister's wife."

Demi sent him a look. "If you have only come to insult me, you may go away again!"

His eyes gleamed with amusement. A slight smile tugged at the corners of his mouth. "You wound me. I have gone out of my way to offer solace, and all you will do is tell me to go away. I must tell you, Miss Standish, I'm not at all accustomed to this sort of treatment. In general I seem to have the opposite effect on women."

Demi didn't know whether to be amused or irritated. Finally, amusement won out. "I had not pegged you as being so full of your own consequence."

He sighed. "It's hard to remain humble when so many designing mamas and dutiful daughters are throwing themselves at your head."

Surprised by the comment, Demi looked him over

searchingly. "I suppose by that you mean that no matter what your station in life, there are always obstacles to one's happiness. *You*, at least, have the option of running, however."

"But that wounds my dignity," he said pensively.

She chuckled in spite of herself. "I'll admit I have trouble imagining it."

"Would you run if you could?"

Demi shrugged. "I'm certain I will grow accustomed," she said, not very convincingly.

"I take it by that the answer is no. There are no other options?"

She turned to study him again. She'd been at pains not to admit how distasteful she found her engagement, but she supposed it would've been obvious to a stump that she was unhappy about it. "None that I would seriously consider. None that are not as bad or worse."

"You've no sense of adventure then?" he said, smiling faintly.

She sighed. "Aunt Alma has always accused me of being just like my father whenever I displease her, but I'm afraid I'm not as much like my father she seems to think--no, I don't. I have far too much imagination."

"Some would say being adventuresome requires an imagination."

"A fanciful imagination, I should think," Demi said tartly. "For myself, I am more inclined to imagine the consequences of rash actions."

"You have a particular reason for not wishing to wed Reverend Flemming?"

"Beyond the fact that I would be trading one tyrant for another far more dangerous one?" Demi responded tartly, then gasped and covered her mouth with her hand, looking at him wide-eyed. "I should not have said that. I don't know what made me say that."

Lord Wyndham was frowning. "The fact that you believe it to be true?"

She sighed. "You don't? I mean, do you think that I've misjudged him?"

Again, he shrugged. "You would be in a better position to judge than I."

Demi huddled a little deeper into his coat and

shivered. The sun had set and long shadows spilled into the meadow from the wood that surrounded it. It would be dark soon. She knew she should go in, but she was reluctant to return to Moreland Abbey and the almost certain wrath of her aunt. As if he sensed her thoughts, or perhaps because she'd shivered, Lord Wyndham slipped an arm around her shoulders and pulled her close. She stiffened, but she didn't try to pull away. After a few moments, she relaxed against him, dropping her head against his shoulder, relishing her closeness to him.

She knew he meant to kiss her when he tucked a finger beneath her chin and urged her to look up at him.

She knew she shouldn't allow it.

She lifted her face to look up at him without hesitation, with complete trust. Their gazes locked for a suspended moment in time, then, slowly, he dipped his head closer to hers, brushed his lips lightly across the sensitive surfaces of her own. A rush of delight filled her at the feather light contact, suspending her breath in her chest. When he lifted his head slightly to look into her eyes, she held herself perfectly still, waiting to see what he would do next.

He released a sharp exhalation from his chest as she met his gaze, as if he, too, had been holding his breath. Something flickered in his eyes, surprise and something more, something dark, heated. Slipping his hand from her chin to the base of her skull, he lowered his head once more, pressing his lips to hers and releasing, and then moving ever so slightly and molding his lips against hers again, as if seeking the perfect fit. An intoxicating lethargy swept through Demi at his light caresses, as his breath mingled with her own. Lifting a hand, she caught a fistful of his shirt above his pounding heart and moved closer.

Lightly, he touched the seam where her lips met with the tip of his tongue. A ripple of surprise went through Demi, a touch of doubt. She subdued it. Hesitantly, she parted her lips, not entirely certain that that was what he wanted, but willing to allow him to do what he would with her. He opened his mouth over hers then, thrusting his tongue past the lax barrier of her lips and teeth and raking it along her own. A jolt went through her at the unaccustomed contact that was part surprise and part something else she couldn't begin to define. Like the spirits she'd drank from the flask, it sent a wave of dizziness through her and created a warm, melting sensation inside of her, evoking a frantic rhythm from her heart. Briefly, she wavered between fear of the unknown and the desire to see where he would lead her. Desire won out, and she relaxed against him, savoring his possession, submerging herself completely in the unaccustomed sensations creating havoc within her as he explored her mouth thoroughly, caressing her in a way she would never have imagined allowing any man, let alone wanting.

She did want it, though. The sensations enthralled her as much as they confused her and when he began to withdraw, she leaned closer, thrusting her tongue into his mouth to explore as he had explored hers. A shudder went through him, but before she could retreat in her uncertainty over his reaction to her boldness, he closed his mouth around her tongue and sucked. It sent a hard jolt of fire through her veins, draining the strength from her so that she felt weak all over.

Abruptly, he broke the kiss. Disappointment instantly flooded her. With an effort, she lifted her lids to look up at him reproachfully. He stared back at her for a long moment, his face taut, unyielding. Finally, he tucked her head against his shoulder, stroking a shaking hand along her shoulder and down her arm. "Don't look at me like that," he said hoarsely, "unless you're of a mind to have your skirts tossed over your head."

She stiffened. After a moment, she pulled away from him, trying to sort through her chaotic feelings. She knew very well that she should have been outraged at the comment. Somehow, though, she was more intrigued by it than insulted.

He released her, scrubbed a hand over his face and shifted uncomfortably, straightening one leg. She looked him over curiously. "You have a muscle cramp?"

The question startled a chuckle out of him. He turned and studied her a long moment. Finally, he took her hand and, watching her face, pressed her open hand against his lower belly, sliding her palm over a long, hard ridge of flesh that she hadn't noticed before. Comprehension dawned almost instantaneously, however. She'd spent much of her life in the country, certainly enough to have a fairly firm grasp on the concept of mating between animals. She just hadn't, previously, considered there might be a similarity between humans and animals. "Oh." She felt her face redden and jerked her hand back.

Settling back, she stared down at her hand in the deepening twilight. She could still feel the impression along her palm, the heat of it, a faint pulsing of life. Her belly clenched as she stared at her hand and she curled her fingers inward. She knew she shouldn't pursue it further, shouldn't have pursued it as far as she had, but she discovered a burning need to know if it was in any way significant for him as it had been for her.

She was not in the habit of allowing men to kiss her, although she knew Phoebe had experimented with kissing more than once. She had not, in point of fact, had either the opportunity or the desire to do so before. "Does it … does that always happen?"

He sent her a sharp glance. "You should never ask a man a question like that, my dear, if you expect him to treat you like a lady."

The rebuke was certainly warranted. It stung nevertheless. She nodded. "I expect I shall discover it for myself soon enough," she muttered to herself, revolted at the idea of discovering something like that in Jonathan Flemming's breeches when he kissed her. Would it be that big, she wondered? Or would it be bigger still, since he was a bigger man than Lord Wyndham? The thought sent a wave of panic through her. She knew it was supposed to fit inside of her, she had just never quite figured out where.

Beside her, Lord Wyndham stiffened, and she realized, belatedly, that she must have muttered her thoughts aloud. "I should go in now," she said quickly, pulling his coat from her shoulders and handing it back to him. "Thank you."

He took it, and stood up, pulling her to her feet.

Peering up at him, she saw that he was still angry, far more angry than she'd realized. She was sorry for it, but would it be better to apologize for her brazen manners, she wondered? Or would it be best to try to pretend that it had never happened?

She stared down at her hands a moment. "You are so ... comfortable to talk to. I apologize if I made you uncomfortable after your kindness to me."

He caught her shoulders when she would have turned away. She looked up at him in surprise. "You should not get too comfortable with me, Demi. It would be all too easy for me to forget that I am a gentleman and you are lady, particularly when you kiss me like that."

She grimaced. "I shouldn't have kissed you back?"

He shook his head slowly, moving closer. Catching her arms, he placed them around his neck, pulling her tightly against him. "No," he murmured, leaning close and brushing his lips against hers lightly once more. "Nor allowed me to kiss you the way I did."

"Why?" Demi asked breathlessly when his lips parted from hers briefly.

"Because now I know what you do to me ... and what I do to you ... instead of merely imagining what it would feel like to kiss you," he said between short, nibbling kisses. "And now I have a burning need to discover what it would be like to make love to you."

He kissed her deeply then, as he had before, but with far less restraint. Her belly clenched as excitement washed through her. Heat burgeoned instantly inside of her, where before it had grown slowly from warmth to fire. Dizzy, breathless, she rose up on her toes and tightened her arms around his neck, caressing his tongue with her own and finally sucking on it as he had hers before. He groaned, slipping a hand down along her back and cupping her buttocks through her gown, pressing her lower body tightly against his own. The swollen ridge of flesh was bruisingly hard, but she imitated his movements, rocking her hips against his.

He squeezed her buttocks tightly, holding her still as he tore his lips from hers and buried his face along the crook of her neck, breathing raggedly. Finally, he set her away from him. She looked at him doubtfully, confused that he'd pushed her away.

"Go inside, Demi," he said harshly. "Now!"

She took a step back at the growled order and finally turned and fled.

Chapter Four

Luck was not something Demi had more than a
passing familiarity with, but for once it came to her
rescue. She managed to make it into the house and up
the servant's stairs without encountering anyone. Her
maid, Sarah, was in her room when Demi dashed inside
and bolted the door behind her. Dragging in a
shuddering breath of relief, Demi leaned back against
the door, her eyes closed tightly.

"Ye look as if ye've seen a ghost."

Demi opened her eyes and stared at her maid,
repressing a hysterical urge to giggle nervously. "A
dragon more like. I thought sure Aunt Alma would meet
me on the way up."

Sarah moved across the room, a finger to her lips.
"Ye've only missed her by a hair," she said quietly.
"How did ye manage to get by without her seeing you?"

Demi grimaced. "I sneaked up the backstairs. I ... uh
... was ill. I went out to the necessary."

Sarah eyed her suspiciously. "An' stopped by yer dear
departed uncle's cellaret on the way back from the
smell of ye," she responded tartly, leaning a little closer
and sniffing.

Clapping a hand to her mouth, Demi's eyes widened.
"You can smell it!" she gasped in horror. "I only had a
sip."

Sarah nodded. "An' I suppose ye had no more than a
toke of one of his cigars while ye was at it?"

"Good God!" Demi exclaimed, fighting the rising tide
of hysteria inside of her. "Help me change! Quickly!
Aunt Alma has the nose of a bloodhound. If you can
smell it, she certainly will."

Without another word, Sarah helped her strip her
gown and shift off, bundling them into a ball as Demi
rushed to the wash stand and quickly bathed her face
and hands with soap. When she turned, Sarah was
holding out a linen hand towel. "Ye've the look of a

maiden that's been thoroughly kissed, if you don't mind my saying so," she commented, "and the smell of him on yer clothes."

Demi pressed her hands to her cheeks. "Have I?" she asked self-consciously.

Sarah nodded. "I'm thinkin' it weren't the Reverend Flemming, neither. He was that put out when he left a bit ago."

Demi moved to the bed and sat down weakly on the edge of the mattress. "Aunt Alma will be furious with me.... He didn't.... You don't think he called off the engagement, do you?"

Sarah studied her curiously for several moments. "I've a notion I would've been belting back a bit o' the hard stuff if I found meself tied to that one. An' I'm thinkin' ye agree with me on it. Would ye be that displeased if he did?"

Demi covered her face with her hands, feeling the urge to weep sweep over her. With an effort, she swallowed the knot of misery. "It's not a matter of what I want. It's what Aunt Alma wants, and what he wants. I don't have a choice .... Aunt Alma all but said plain out that she would disown me if I refused his offer. And I've got no where to go!"

Frowning, Sarah moved across the room. Dropping the bundle of clothing near the door, she went to the armoire and pulled a nightgown out for her mistress, then returned and helped her remove her corset and slip the gown on. "What about Lord Wyndham?"

Demi glanced at her sharply. "Lord Wyndham," she echoed faintly.

Sarah gave her a look. "It was him ye met in the garden, weren't it? I've seen the sheep's eyes you been castin' his way for the past six months and more, and the look on your face whenever his name's mentioned."

Blood climbed into Demi's cheeks. She looked at Sarah in dismay. "I've been that obvious?"

Sarah smiled faintly. "Ye've no need to worry anyone else noticed ... except his lordship himself, that is. There ain't a soul in this household that ever notices anything beyond their own nose."

Demi felt only marginally better. "I'm sure he didn't

notice. I never once even glanced his way when he was looking in my direction."

Sarah chuckled. "It's been almost comical to watch the two of you going to such pains *not* to glance at each other. Lord Wyndham'd be lougin' against a wall, or sprawled all casual-like in a chair, watching your every move like a big, sleepy cat ready to pounce and gobble you up the moment you came close enough. An' you flutterin' all nervous around the room, like the little bird that knows that old cat's just waitin' for you to make the wrong move."

Demi blushed all over again, but frowned as she crawled into her bed and pulled the covers up. "You're just saying that," she said, doubt and hope warring for dominance.

"I wouldn't say it if I didn't know it was true," Sarah assured her, dampening a towel in the washbowl and then moving to the small fire on the hearth and holding the cloth out to catch the heat. "I've been around enough to know what that look in a man's eyes means."

Demi sighed, stilling the nervous fluttering of her heart with an effort, but she forced a smile. "I'm glad you told me. At least that's something … even though … even though nothing could ever come of it."

Sarah's brows rose. "Why would nothing come of it? He's taken a fancy to you. You've taken a fancy to him."

Demi shook her head. "He's a peer of the realm, Sarah. I'm … a nobody and as poor as a church mouse. It wouldn't be a suitable match. I know it, and he knows it, too, I can assure you."

Sarah flipped the towel over, fanning it. "He's poor, too?"

Demi grimaced. "I don't think so. Aunt Alma wouldn't let him near her precious Phoebe if he was. At any rate, if he was, it would be even more unsuitable, for then he'd *have* to marry a woman of wealth. What are you doing, anyway?"

Sarah grinned. "Yer aunt'll be back. I'm thinkin' she'll be less inclined to linger if yer hot and flushed."

Demi stared at the cloth for several moments while that comment slowly sank in. Almost as if on cue, she heard someone coming along the hallway. Signaling frantically for the cloth, Demi pressed it to her face and lay back, listening intently. She knew almost immediately that it was her aunt. It seemed doubtful she would knock. She wasn't in the habit of doing so at any time, and she was convinced Demi was up to something tonight. The moment the footsteps paused outside her door, Demi snatched the cloth off her face and shoved it under the covers.

The door flew open. Demi raised up slightly, peering through blurred eyes at the door. By the time she'd managed to blink the steaming moisture from her eyes and focus, Alma Moreland's expression had gone from rage to one of suspicion. Stalking across the room, she stared down at Demi for several moments. "I came to check on you. Where have you been?"

Demi licked her dried lips. "I was ill. I went out to the necessary."

Her aunt's lips tightened. After a moment's hesitation, she touched Demi's face. "You may have a touch of fever," she concluded ungraciously. "Mr. Flemming was not at all pleased with your behavior today. He's to call tomorrow to take you on an outing. Unless you're at death's door, I suggest you be ready to greet him with more warmth."

Turning, she stalked from the room and slammed the door behind her.

Sarah glared indignantly at the door, her hands on her hips. "*Might* have a touch of fever? An' yer face as red as blood and hot as fire!"

Demi couldn't help but chuckle. "You know very well I don't have a fever," she said, fishing the damp cloth from beneath her coverlet and handing it to Sarah.

Sarah looked at her, but she didn't seem appeased in the least. "Aye, but *she* didn't, the old battle ax. Yer not goin' to let her push ye into marryin' that man, are ye?"

Demi's amusement vanished. "I don't have a choice."

"His lordship might have somethin' to say to that if someone was to let him know."

Demi swallowed against a sudden lump in her throat. "You're such a romantic, Sarah! He knows."

"But does he know yer sweet on him?"

She blushed. "I think so."

Sarah frowned. "Maybe he only needs a little nudge."

Demi sighed. "Aunt Alma would have me shipped off to the workhouse faster than I could say squat if she suspected for a moment that I was hanging after Phoebe's beau."

"He's not Phoebe's beau, never was. Haven't I been tellin' ye it's you he's had his eye on the whole time. You may be blind, and he might be blind, but I'm not!"

Demi wanted to believe her in the worst kind of way, but, unfortunately, she was more inclined to think her aunt might have been right than Sarah. If he *had* noticed her as Sarah said, then his intentions toward her had almost certainly been dishonorable. If they had been anything else, he would have approached her openly, not clandestinely.

She should have been completely devastated by the knowledge. She was certainly hurt, but there was a bittersweet gladness, as well, that he at least found her attractive on some level. She could've wished for far more, but she was enough of a realist that it had never occurred to her that he might actually court her. She hadn't thought he would notice her at all and she felt a faint stirring of happiness at the realization that he had. Something was better than nothing, to her mind.

Shaking her head, Sarah gathered the bundle of clothes by the door and left. Demi lay back, staring dreamily at the ceiling as she allowed her mind to replay those moments with him in the meadow. She'd been wrong, she realized. Being sick hadn't totally marred the memory. He'd been so kind, so matter of fact about it, that her embarrassment had faded.

And then he'd kissed her and held her. He'd desired her. She couldn't help but wonder what might have happened if she'd ignored his warning and stayed. It made her feel warm all over trying to imagine what he might have done.

She was drifting dreamily when the door opened abruptly. She sat up guiltily, staring at her maid. Sarah was leaning against the door, her hand over her chest.

"What is it?" Demi gasped a little breathlessly.

"I'd thought I might sneak ye a bit to eat up the

backstairs, but yer aunt was layin' in wait for me," she gasped.

Demi bit her lip, trying to curb her amusement at the look on Sarah's face.

"Aye, ye may laugh, but it weren't ye that had a run in with the old battle ax! Gave me a nasty turn, it did!"

"I'm so sorry. It was sweet of you to think of it. I wish you hadn't mentioned it, though. I hardly ate anything at luncheon, and ... well I lost that I was so sick afterwards. Now I'm famished."

Sarah darted away from the door, fishing a biscuit from the pocket of her apron. "Bread and water'll have to hold ye. I lost the rest when Lady Firebreather crept up behind me." Dropping the biscuit in Demi's outstretched hands, she hit for the door again. "If she comes in while yer eatin', yer on yer own."

The moment Sarah disappeared out the door, Demi hopped from the bed and rushed over to latch it. Nibbling on the biscuit, she headed for the pitcher of water on her washstand. She'd just swallowed the last bite and lifted the pitcher for a drink of water when something large and heavy crashed into her door. A loud shriek followed. "Demitria Standish! Open this door instantly!"

Demi almost dropped the pitcher. Swallowing with an effort, she glanced around a little wildly, then, stalling for time, called out weakly, "Is that you, Aunt Alma?"

Her cheeks felt perfectly cool when she touched them. Darting on tiptoe around the bed, she looked around frantically for the cloth she'd used before. Unfortunately, Sarah had gathered it up and taken it with her soiled clothing. Scurrying toward the fireplace, she leaned her face as close to the flames as she dared. Almost instantly, the foul smell of singed hair hit her and she drew back, checking her hair and eyebrows.

"You know very well it's me! Why have you locked the door?"

"I'm coming," Demi called, racing back to the bed and bouncing on it once before landing beside it heavily.

Her aunt was livid when she finally opened the door. Brushing past Demi, she searched the room suspiciously before she whirled to confront her. "Why was the door locked?"

"It was locked?" Demi echoed, but she realized instantly that her aunt wasn't likely to fall for an act of innocence. "My head hurt. I'd forgotten I locked it because I didn't want anyone to wake me."

Alma Moreland's eyes narrowed. "I smell burning hair."

Demi touched her hair self-consciously, wondering if she'd done more than merely singe it. "I was cold. I guess I got a little too close to the fire."

It was clear her aunt didn't believe a word of it, but after a moment she turned to go. "Remember what I said earlier."

Nodding, Demi closed the door, then, feeling a burst of rebelliousness, locked it, making no attempt to slip the bolt home quietly.

Her aunt paused just outside the door, but apparently decided she wasn't in the mood for another confrontation. After a moment, she turned and left.

When she could no longer hear her aunt, Demi returned to the pitcher and drank enough water to wash the dry biscuit down and then crawled into the bed once more. It wasn't until she'd settled that she recalled her aunt's collision with the door. A chuckle escaped her before she thought better of it. Clamping a hand over her mouth, she stifled the peal of laughter that followed the best she could, but each time she thought she'd gotten control over her wayward humor, she'd envision her aunt slamming into her locked door and lose control all over again.

Finally, exhausted, she blew out the lamp beside her bed and settled back. Anxiety almost immediately washed over her, chasing the last of her humor far away. She was to have an outing with Mr. Flemming on the morrow, and she looked forward to that with about as much enthusiasm as she looked forward to facing her aunt.

As it turned, however, her aunt had other things on her mind. Young Lord Moreland arrived from Eton, having been expelled for the remainder of the term.

Chapter Five

Demi was both surprised and relieved when Reverend Flemming arrived the following day with Esme perched up in the carriage beside him. She'd spent the morning in her room, pacing the floor, too nervous to sit for very long at the time and far too nervous to venture downstairs, where she was almost certain to run into someone she'd as soon not.

In the bright light of day, her romantic interlude with Lord Wyndham took on a whole new light. She was dismayed at her own behavior and couldn't help but wonder if the entire episode had been entirely of her making. Lord Wyndham was a gentleman, but when all was said and done, he was still a man. Had he actually instigated the kiss, she wondered now? Or had she been so desperate for his attention that he'd taken his cue from her?

It was mortifying to think that that might have been the case. She didn't know if she could face him again.

She'd been going over and over it in her mind, but try as she might she couldn't recall anything he'd done leading up to that moment, the first kiss, that might have indicated a desire to kiss her, let alone anything more. He'd given her his coat. When she'd begun shivering, she remembered that he'd moved closer and even placed an arm around her shoulders. She'd thought that he was going to kiss her and she'd looked up, hoping he would, but she couldn't remember now why she'd thought so.

She put her hands to her burning cheeks. She'd thrown herself at his head, just as her aunt had accused her of doing, and she didn't have to wonder what he'd thought about it for he'd made indecent suggestions, and she hadn't even had the good sense to at least behave as if she'd been offended!

She'd actually touched 'it', and she hadn't screamed or fainted or even thought to slap his face. She'd *wanted* to touch it. She'd wanted to examine it more than she had.

Someone was bound to have seen them together. There would be talk, a scandal. Jonathan Flemming would withdraw his offer and she'd be ruined and her aunt would ship her off ... somewhere.

She almost jumped out of her skin when a maid tapped at the door to let her know that Mr. Flemming had arrived. "I'll be right down," she responded, hurrying over to grab the bonnet and shawl she'd chosen to go with her outfit. She stopped before the mirror on her dressing table long enough to perch the bonnet on her head and secure it with its ribbons. Her face was pale with fright, but she rather thought after her pretended illness the day before that it was better than bouncing down the stairs with the glow of health in her cheeks.

Tossing the shawl over one arm, she left the room and made her way downstairs. She had to feign surprise at the discovery that Esme would be joining them. She didn't want either her aunt or Mr. Flemming to know that she'd been watching for the carriage from upstairs. Jonathan greeted her a little stiffly, his gaze suspicious as he looked her over and she wondered guiltily if it was because of her bad behavior in the parlor the day before or if he'd seen her in the meadow with Lord Wyndham.

Once they'd settled in the carriage, she discovered why Esme had been included in the outing. Their destination was the small town of Moreland, named for the abbey, rather than vice versa. Their *expressed* reason for going was to see about making a few purchases to furbish Esme's wardrobe and to take luncheon at the local tavern. It wasn't until they'd left the carriage at the livery and begun to stroll through town that Demi realized the true reason for their trip to town. They'd not gone far when one of Reverend Flemming's parishioners stepped from one of the shops they passed and stopped to chat when he tipped his hat at her. "Allow me to introduce my fiancé, Miss Demitria Standish," Flemming said without preamble.

The woman, who looked to be around Flemming's age, looked Demi over and forced a polite smile, offering her hand. "So nice to meet you, my dear. You're Lord Moreland's cousin?"

Demi pasted an artificial smile on her lips and nodded.

They covered several blocks in much the same manner, stopping to greet Flemming's numerous acquaintances, exchange introductions and pleasantries, and then move on again, and finally arrived at the shop that was Esme's goal--which was directly across the street from a livery.

Demi felt like the lowest form of human life during the course of the first several introductions. She'd accepted his offer of marriage when she hadn't wanted him at all, had, in fact fallen head over heels for Lord Wyndham many months ago. Worse, the very night she'd accepted him, she'd been in the meadow with Lord Wyndham doing her utmost to encourage him to lose his head and ... ravish her, and she hadn't felt a whit of shame over it--until now.

It had not occurred to her before that he might honestly feel some affection toward her, that he might be wounded by her perfidy, and his obvious pride in her was almost worse, for she could well imagine what even a hint of scandal would do to him.

It wasn't until she happened to catch the cold glitter of possessiveness in his eyes as he glanced at her that she began to have a totally different picture of the situation and began to entertain grave doubts about her intelligence. He was proud of her, that was for certain, but not for the reasons she'd attributed to him. She was related to the Morelands of Moreland Abby, a poor relation, and not even on the Moreland side, but that didn't seem to matter to any of the people they met, and thus it didn't matter to Flemming either. She could see the calculating looks in their eyes as well as Flemming's, and knew that they were speculating on how much had been settled on her.

By the time they reached the shop, she'd tilted in the other direction once more and begun to wonder if she'd misjudged Flemming. Was it her sense of guilt and shame that had made her feel she had to have an excuse for her behavior? Her dislike of the match that made her want to find fault in him? She could not think that

Flemming behaved the least bit as if he was enamored with her, but perhaps that was only because of his position in the community? Maybe he truly had developed an affection for her and his pride stemmed from that?

Try though she might to be both honest and fair, she didn't believe it. She'd known from the beginning that he was very like her Aunt Alma, and this was just the sort of calculating maneuver that she would consider-- blocking any chance of retreat by the threat of public humiliation. He had very calculatingly introduced her to half the town as his fiancé. By bedtime not a soul in the small hamlet would be unaware of it. If she even considered trying to back out of the engagement now, she would be ruined, her reputation in shambles. Of course, he too would be humiliated, but it was obviously a risk he was willing to take to ensure she didn't try to wiggle out of the deal he and her aunt had hatched between them.

Perhaps a part of it had been aimed at his parishioners themselves, to put them in their place, for it was a well known fact that every widow for miles around had been hanging after him for years and everyone had wondered aloud why he had not married again. He had set out to show them that he was above their touch, a member of the aristocracy. He might not have the breeding or wealth to seek a wife in the highest echelons, but he would have a genteel wife, nevertheless, not the wealthy widow of a merchant.

She could not fault him for having pride in his family name, nor wishing to marry into the peerage when he was genteel himself. His first wife *had* been a wealthy merchant's daughter and she supposed it must have chafed so proud a man to know that everyone considered that he'd been forced to marry beneath him because his pocketbook required it.

It did not make her feel more kindly toward him. She'd hoped, since she had no choice in the matter, that she might find something that would appeal to her. Instead, it seemed the more familiar she became with him, the worse her prospects of happiness looked.

Apparently, he sensed the dislike she was trying hard

to hide, or better yet, dismiss. Once he'd finished parading her about town, he set out to charm her. The luncheon the three of them shared was almost pleasant, and not entirely due to Esme's presence, though Esme was so excited about the rare treat that it was infectious. By the time they set out for the return trip to Moreland Abby, Demi was almost relaxed--right up until the moment that she realized that they had detoured by the parsonage to drop Esme off before returning her home.

She glanced at Flemming uneasily as the door closed behind Esme and forced a nervous smile. "I expect Aunt Alma will begin to wonder if we have had a carriage accident we have been gone so long."

Flemming sent her a cool smile. "I told her that we would most likely be late."

"Oh?" Demi responded a little uneasily. "I am quite certain she will have expected us back by now, though. We generally dine early unless we're having guests and Aunt Alma is a stickler for punctuality."

Jonathan sent her a speculative glance and flicked the reins. "Soon or late, she will have to grow accustomed to the fact that, as your husband, I will expect to have a say in your comings and goings. At any rate, I'm sure she'll forgive us if we're a little late."

Demi caught her bonnet with one hand and the armrest at the edge of the seat with the other as the carriage jolted forward. "I expect she will concede that … once we are wed, but then there is no telling with Aunt Alma. She is very accustomed to having her way." She frowned as his body bumped her side and his arm brushed along hers for the third time in less than three minutes. Glancing down at the seat between them, she hadn't noticed before that the seat was so narrow that he could not drive without brushing against her. Surreptitiously, she shifted over to put some distance between them.

"We are the next thing to wed now," he said with a complacent smile. "And I am very accustomed to having my own way, as well, particularly where it pertains to my wife."

Demi returned his smile with a slightly forced one. "We are barely engaged as yet and many months from being married."

He shrugged. "The settlements are signed. I'd forgotten you left yesterday before we'd finished up. At any rate, I see no sense in a prolonged engagement, particularly when I am anxious to have you in my home. Your aunt and I settled it between us that we would publish the bans next month and wed the following month."

A jolt of surprise and dismay went through her. She couldn't decide what to respond to first, the fact that Jonathan and her aunt had not only made all the plans, but settled them, as well, without consulting her or even advising her of them. Or his statement that the contracts had been signed without her. "The contracts can not be signed. I did not sign."

"Your aunt took the liberty of signing for you since you weren't feeling well. She is your legal guardian, after all."

It was on the tip of her tongue to inform her that her aunt could also take the liberty of marrying him and taking her place in the marriage bed if she was so anxious to do it all. "Don't you think announcing the engagement and following it by a wedding within two months is scandalously precipitous? People are bound to think the worst. I'd expected we would be engaged a year, at least, before we began to discuss a wedding."

He sent her a look of surprise. "Did you? But we were discussing the wedding plans when you left yesterday. Surely you must have realized that we would not be planning it a year in advance. In any case, I've no wish for a prolonged engagement. We are all in agreement. We have known each other since you first arrived at Moreland Abbey."

"I was scarcely eight years old!" Demi exclaimed in outrage.

"Exactly my point. I have known you nigh ten years now. I watched you grow up from a pretty little girl to a beautiful woman. I am anxious to have you for my wife."

Demi felt a little nauseated. Put that way, she had to wonder if he'd had his eye on her since that time. She supposed some women might find that romantic. She might have herself, for that matter, if she had felt any sort of affection for him. She didn't, and she began to wonder if she could manage even to tolerate him when she was being forced from every direction without regard to her sensibilities. She thought she might adjust, if given time. She might even learn acceptance, but every feeling revolted at being pitched so precipitously into the most extreme intimacy with a man she felt she already knew better than she wanted to.

She surfaced from her introspection just as the carriage took a fork off of the main road. "Where are we going?" she asked a little blankly.

"I thought perhaps we could drive down to the lake and have a few moments to ourselves before I took you home."

"But ... we have been gone all day. Perhaps we could do this another time? I'm really very tired now."

"We won't stay long."

A combination of fear and anger washed through Demi. Her lips tightened, but she didn't trust herself to speak. He drew the carriage to a halt at last before the lake. She folded her arms over her chest and stared angrily at the water while he set the hand brake and looped he reins around it.

"You are angry," he observed coolly.

"You are observant," she snapped.

He settled back in his seat and stretched his long legs out, propping them on the dashboard. Demi stared daggers at the toes of his boots and twisted in the seat, putting her back to him. He slid a hand around her waist and dragged her back against him before she even realized his intent, dropping his chin on her shoulder. "I'd only thought we might share a few private moments," he murmured huskily next to her ear.

A shiver went through her as his hot breath fanned the side of her neck. "Let go of me then, and we'll talk."

He chuckled, dragging her onto his lap. "Talking isn't what I had in mind."

Demi gaped at him, too shocked at his audacity to think of a response. He took advantage of her defenselessness, covering her mouth with his own ... also her chin and the tip of her nose. The sense of suffocation was instantaneous and she planted her palms against his chest, twisting her head, struggling to pull free. His arms tightened around her, but she managed to free her airway and dragged in a breath of air, clamping her teeth tightly as she felt his tongue snake out, demanding entrance. He forced her jaws apart despite all she could do, throttling her with his tongue, drowning her with a wash of saliva so that she could think of nothing but escape.

Her gyrations only seemed to excite him. As she twisted in his lap, a rod of flesh hardened beneath her thigh. He released her mouth almost as abruptly as he'd captured it. For perhaps a second, Demi thought he would release her altogether. Then, he fastened his mouth against her throat and began to work a slimy trial downward. She put the heel of her palm against his forehead, trying to thrust him away, without any discernible effect. Twisting her head, she glanced around frantically for something to club him with.

Not surprisingly, she saw nothing. She hadn't even thought to bring a parasol since it was early spring yet and the sun far too cool to warrant one. The hand brake caught her eye, however, and she struggled to reach it, just brushing it with the tips of her fingers. Frustrated, she dug her heels into the seat and thrust backward. He took the opportunity to fasten his mouth over her breast. Moisture saturated the gown instantly and even through the fabric she could feel his teeth and tongue as he raked them against her nipple.

Ignoring him, she grasped the hand brake and snatched it back. The horse, already agitated by the struggle in the carriage, jolted forward.

Releasing her abruptly, Jonathan dumped her onto the seat and grabbed for the reins. Setting the brake once more, he draped the reins around it again. When he turned, his eyes were glazed, dark, predatory. Grasping Demi, he tugged her hips across the seat toward him, pushing her backwards at the same time so that she fell back against the seat. Sprawling half on top of her, he covered her mouth in another drowning kiss. As he wedged a knee between her legs, freeing one from beneath his body, she kicked wildly at the hand brake, finally knocking it backward once more.

Again, the horse jogged forward, jolting the carriage. The motion overbalanced their precarious position and Jonathan rolled into the floorboard, taking her with him. He released her instantly, however, struggling to catch the reins. Demi pushed herself upright, very deliberately planted her knee on top of his engorged manhood and focused her entire weight on it as she struggled to crawl up on the seat once more. He let out a bellow of pain and rage and jackknifed upright as she scrambled off of him.

"Oh!" she exclaimed, striving to compose her features into a look of concern. "Did I hurt you?"

He sent her a glare and concentrated on catching the reins and halting the horse once more. The pain seemed to have cooled his ardor, however, if not his temper. He settled in the seat and raked a hand through his mussed hair. "No," he answered finally. "I bumped my ... knee."

Shaking like a leaf, Demi concentrated on straightening her gown. He handed her her shawl wordlessly, and she wrapped it around her shoulders. She'd lost the pin she had used to pin it over her less than modest neckline. The gown was torn where he'd pulled it loose. She folded the shawl over it and held it tightly to her. "I'm a little chilled," she said after a moment when he merely sat, staring at her speculatively.

Without a word, he flicked the reins and turned the carriage, heading back down the lane they'd taken to the lake. As the fear began to subside, Demi realized she'd lost half her hair pins, as well. Releasing the shawl, she made a half hearted effort to straighten her hair and finally merely stuffed the wayward tendrils under her bonnet and tied the ribbons more tightly under her chin.

By the time they'd reached Moreland Abby, anger had replaced her fear. The moment the carriage rocked to a halt, Demi leapt down and stomped into the house without a word or a glance in Jonathan's direction. She was half way up the walk when he caught up to her, grasping her upper arm. She was still trying to pull free when Jonathan brought her to a halt in front of the dining room. To her surprise, he released her abruptly.

She saw why when she turned. Her aunt, seated at the opposite end of the table, was gaping at them with every appearance of shock. Since Demi had no doubt at all that she looked as if she'd been mauled, she wasn't the least surprised. The bodice of her gown was torn, her hair falling down all around her shoulders and her face chafed from whisker burn. She glared at her aunt. "I will *not* marry this man! Throw me into the street! I don't care!"

"Demitria Standish!" Alma Moreland roared, coming to her feet. "We have company!"

Demi noticed then that her cousin, Geoffrey, was seated at the head of the table. Ranged around the table were two of Phoebe's particular friends and two gentlemen. One of them was Lord Wyndham. He was staring directly at her and Jonathan, his eyes narrowed, his face taut.

"What is the meaning of this disgraceful display?"

Demi glanced from her aunt to Flemming. Far from looking the least bit discomfited, he wore a half smile of triumph, his gaze locked with Lord Wyndham's. It coalesced in Demi's mind on the instant that she'd been set up by Flemming and her aunt. It was pure speculation, of course. It might also have been nothing more than a dislike of both of them, but it seemed a bit too convenient that they'd managed to arrive, in a disheveled manner that practically screamed fornication, to discover the dining room full of witnesses. And now that she thought on it, the doors were never left open while they were dining. Why now, unless her aunt had been anticipating her to arrive home looking as if she'd spent the day making love?

"The man can not drive!" she exclaimed on sudden inspiration. "I was nearly thrown from the carriage and killed, and all because he decided to drop Esme off before bringing me to the Abbey and thought we should drive faster to account for it!"

Something gleamed in Lord Wyndham's eyes, approval she thought, but both her aunt and Flemming looked as if they might burst a blood vessel. Phoebe and her friends tittered nervously, obviously as scandalized as they had been intended to be.

Demi didn't delude herself. Despite the story inspired by desperation, she knew very well that speculation would be rife and running through the county like wildfire before morning. Whether her aunt and Flemming had conspired against her or not, even if Flemming had only been inspired by the moment and had not planned it, she was ruined just the same. If she married him, the scandal would eventually die down-- once the whole county had counted the months until the delivery of her first child and been disappointed by the fact that it did not arrive early. If she did not marry him, she would not get another decent proposal, even if her aunt decided to allow her to remain under her roof.

"Excuse me," she muttered abruptly. Brushing past Flemming, she raced up the stairs. When she reached her room, she slammed the door and bolted it behind her.

Still weak and shaken from her experience, her body urged her to collapse on the bed, but nerves and fury drove her to pace back and forth instead. Finally, she moved to her dressing table. The tear in her bodice was not too noticeable and, perhaps, they'd overlooked it. On the other hand, her gown was as crumpled as if she'd slept in it. Her bonnet was askew, and her hair was tangled and falling down all about her head. As she suspected, her cheeks were red from the abrasion of Flemming's whiskers as he'd gnawed her face.

Shuddering at the realization that she could smell him on her skin, she went to the wash stand and washed her mouth out, then scrubbed her face and hands with soap. A tentative knock sounded at her door while she was in the process of washing. She lifted her head. "Who is it?"

"It's me, Miss. Sarah."

Grabbing a hand towel, Demi moved toward the door. "Are you alone?" she asked cautiously before she unbolted the door.

"Yes, Miss."

Demi put her ear to the door, but could discern no sound that might indicate otherwise. Finally, she unbolted the door, grasped Sarah's wrist and snatched her inside. She bolted the door again before she turned to her maid. "Help me undress, please."

Sarah looked her over anxiously, but forbore comment, merely nodding and reaching for the closure at the back of the gown.

When she'd stripped down to her pantalets and corset, she ordered Sarah to take the clothing out and burn it. "I don't ever want to see it again."

Sarah gathered the clothing into a ball, studying Demi worriedly. "Is it true then? The Reverend ravished you?"

Demi stared at her, feeling blood surge up her neck and flood her face. "*No!* It is not true! Although he most certainly had it in mind."

Sarah looked relieved but still troubled. "There's bound to be a horrible scandal. They're sayin' downstairs that you should never have accepted his proposal in the first place if you didn't want to marry him, that you'll *have* to marry him now, an' the sooner the better--before your belly starts a swellin'."

Chapter Six

So much for the clever story she'd cooked up, Demi thought morosely, but then she'd known no one would believe it when there was a much more scandalous possibility they might consider.

When Sarah had left, she'd bolted the door again and pulled a nightgown out to wear. She supposed she really ought to go back downstairs and try to brazen it out, but she simply was not up to it at the moment.

She'd been far more angered and revolted by Flemming's amorous designs than she had been frightened, but the entire incident had been more than a little unsettling. She doubted, in any case, that going downstairs would do anything more than prevent them from talking about her behind her back. They were just as likely to pump her for the gory details as they were to refrain from discussing it because she was present.

In any case, she had not heard any carriages leave and she thought Flemming might still be downstairs. Of a certainty, the others were.

She didn't think she could face Lord Wyndham.

In truth, whatever occurred between her and her fiancé was no one else's business, but she'd comported herself with a complete lack of restraint with Lord Wyndham only the night before. And now she'd arrived home with every appearance of having done the same, or worse.

He must think that she was no more than a trollop.

She felt as if she'd betrayed him with Flemming rather than the other way around. It didn't matter that she had it backwards. That was the way she felt.

When a tap came at her door again, she nearly jumped out of her skin. "Who is it?"

"Sarah."

She moved to the door, listened for a moment and finally opened it. Sarah rushed inside, balancing a tray. Bolting the door, Demi surveyed the offering without enthusiasm. "I'm not hungry."

Ignoring her, Sarah moved to a table and set the tray down. "You should eat."

"I'm too nervous to eat."

Sarah turned and fixed her with a stern look. "A hunger strike isn't likely to help matters a whit. Like as not, you'll faint, and that'll only feed the wagging tongues."

Sighing irritably, Demi sat and nibbled at the food. "Has Reverend Flemming left?"

Sarah made a face. "He's holed up in the study with yer aunt. Lord Geoffrey, Lord Wyndham and Mr. Collins went round to the stables a bit ago, not long after you came in. I heard them say something about going shooting in the morning with Mr. Smythe and Mr. Fairlane ... them's cronies of Lord Geoffrey from Eton. Seems the lot of them got up to something and got themselves expelled. They wasn't too keen on heading for home afterwards, so they came home with Lord Geoffrey for a visit, to rusticate, they called it. Miss Phoebe's in the front parlor with Miss Charlotte and Miss Horatia, though ... if you feel up to a bit of company."

Horatia Wynthrope was probably the biggest gossip in all of England. How fortuitous that she'd been at Moreland Abbey to witness Demi's downfall! "On second thought, I believe I won't go down again this evening. I'd thought, maybe, it would help if I did, but Horatia Wynthrope will only pump me for information and then twist everything I say."

"I expect you're right, but they'll be leaving soon, and probably Reverend Flemming too. You'd best barricade your door if you mean to keep Lady Moreland out."

Demi smiled wearily. "Thanks for the suggestion."

Sarah moved to the door but paused when she reached it. "It's not my place to say so, Miss, but you're liable to find yerself locked in if you think to stay holed up in here long."

Demi, who'd risen to lock the door behind her maid, hesitated but finally nodded. "She's liable to lock me in anyway, for fear I'll slip the noose. I'd leave tonight if I had anywhere to go. Unfortunately, I can't think of anyone that would take me in, especially not now."

She was propped up in bed, waiting, when her aunt arrived at her door several hours later to ring a peal over her for her 'disgraceful behavior'. It took an effort, but Demi bit her tongue and endured, tuning out most of it. Eventually, she ran out of steam and left, but not before she'd emphasized at least a dozen times that Demi had 'burned her bridges' and needn't think she had any alternative other than marrying Mr. Flemming as quickly as could be decently arranged.

She didn't bother to point out that that would only feed the gossip mills. Alma Moreland could hardly be unaware that such actions would only be feeding the fire.

She resolved, however, that whether she was forced to marry the man or not, she had no intention of seeing him again until that time unless she simply couldn't avoid an encounter.

After an anxious night, most of which was spent tossing and turning, she rose early, dressed and went downstairs. Her aunt and her cousin generally broke their fast in bed before they came down and the house was as silent as a tomb when she reached the breakfast parlor. She found it empty, Geoffrey and his cronies apparently already having departed to go shooting. The maid, clearing away the remains of their breakfast, returned with a plate and she settled down to eat in blessed solitude.

When she'd finished, she went into the library, found a book, and left the house for the solitude of the garden. She was tempted to go further afield, but if Geoffrey was out shooting, she thought it safest to stay near the abbey. The boy--young man--had always been a menace with a gun. He was eighteen now, but she sincerely doubted he'd improved since the day he'd shot his gamekeeper in the buttocks with bird shot.

She heard a carriage arrive shortly before noon. Her belly clenched. She knew it must be Mr. Flemming. Resolutely, she ignored sounds of an arrival. She might have to marry him, but they would have to bind and gag her to get her into another carriage with him in the meantime.

The sounds filtering to her from the house escalated

and she frowned. She couldn't imagine Jonathan Flemming arousing such a flap. Finally, curiosity overcame caution and she made her way inside, drawn by the babble of excited voices to the front hall.

Her heart nearly stopped in her chest when she saw the mayhem there. Phoebe was wailing almost hysterically and Lady Moreland looked as if she might faint dead away at any moment. Geoffrey was being supported by two of friends. Blood streamed from his hand, dripping onto the tiles of the hall.

She wondered, without a great deal of sympathy, if the fool had shot his hand off loading his gun. Before she could decide whether to surge forward and offer help, or retreat and leave them to their own devices, several more men struggled through the front door, carrying Lord Wyndham, who was either unconscious ... or dead.

A wave of such horror washed over her that she sank weakly to the floor. She didn't breathe for several moments. It was only as she gasped in a desperate draft of air that she realized she'd been holding her breath as they crossed the hall with his limp form.

She regained her feet as they started up the stairs with him and rushed over. "Is he ... is he...?" She stammered.

"He is unconscious at the moment, Miss Demitria," the man following the procession announced. "I would like to have him comfortably settled before he comes around."

Demi nodded jerkily and led the way up the stairs, throwing open the door to the first guest room they came to and rushing ahead of them to turn the coverlet down.

The man who'd spoken to her, she discovered, was his manservant. When he'd seen to it that Lord Wyndham was settled with utmost care upon the mattress, he turned to her once more. "We'll need to undress him now, Miss."

Demi tore her gaze from Lord Wyndham's pale face to look at the man blankly.

"If you would step outside, Miss? You may return once we have him comfortably settled and stay with him until the surgeon arrives."

Nodding numbly, Demi left the room, leaning weakly against the door for several moments after she'd closed it.

Geoffrey, still supported by his friends and now trailed by Lady Moreland and Phoebe, was hobbling up the stairs. The procession passed her without even glancing in her direction.

She heard cursing in the room behind her and jerked away from the door as if she'd been scalded. A few moments later, the manservant opened the door and ushered the men out who'd brought Lord Wyndham up. "His lordship will see you now, Miss," he said when the men had departed.

"How bad is it?" Demi gasped fearfully.

"I'm no surgeon, Miss Demitria. He seems to have caught the shot in the muscle of his calf, however. Thankfully, his boot prevented a great deal of damage and there does not seem to be an excessive amount of bleeding. I feel most hopeful that the wound will not prove to be mortal."

Demi thought for several moments that she would faint at the mention of mortality. Gripping the edge of the door frame, she fought it off and, after a moment, moved inside. Lord Wyndham was propped against a mound of pillows. The coverlet that had been spread over him was tented at the foot, as if his leg had been propped up on pillows, as well. He was pale, his features taut from pain. Hesitantly, she moved around the bed to the side nearest him and stared down at him, fighting the urge to burst into tears. Something touched the back of her knees and she turned to see that the servant had brought a chair. She stared down at it as if she'd never seen one before.

"You should sit. I'm fairly certain it would not please his lordship if you were to faint and fall."

Demi nodded jerkily and sat, turning to look at Lord Wyndham again. His eyes were closed, but she couldn't tell if he'd lost consciousness again or if he was simply in too much pain to do otherwise. She moistened her fear-dried lips, trying to think of something to say. It seemed like a very poor time to ask what had happened and in any case she could surmise the gist of it. Undoubtedly, he'd fallen victim to Geoffrey's prowess with a gun.

She felt a wave a guilt that she hadn't warned him, that she'd been too caught up in her own concerns to think of his safety.

Almost as if he'd read her mind, he opened his eyes just then. "He fell and the gun discharged," he said tightly. "A stupid accident, no more."

"I will see to it that it is reported as such," the manservant responded.

Demi glanced from one man to the other and slid to the edge of her seat. "You will be able to tell them yourself once you're better."

He studied her a long moment. "I will not feel like answering questions in the meanwhile, however."

Demi nodded jerkily in agreement, but she did not like the trend of the conversation. "Is there anything I can do?"

He forced a wry smile. "You may go so that I won't feel the need to be so manful about it and can gnash my teeth and curse."

Demi jumped to her feet. Before she could rush away, however, he caught her hand.

"That was an attempt at humor."

She swallowed with an effort. "No. I'm not offended. I know it must be near unbearable. I'll come back when you're feeling a little better."

His hand tightened on hers. "Stay. I'd as soon have something to keep my mind off the surgeon."

She glanced at the manservant, wondering if it would be better if she stayed or left. He nodded and left the room, closing the door carefully behind him.

"Your aunt is liable to have apoplexy if she finds you here. Perhaps you should go after all."

He did not release her hand, however, and Demi made no attempt to retrieve it. She shook her head. "Shhh. Don't try to talk and don't worry about me. I doubt Aunt Alma has any notion of where I am or cares, at least for the moment. They brought Geoffrey in bleeding, as well. His hand was injured, and he was limping, but I do not believe that he is hurt very badly.

Regardless, Aunt Alma is bound to coddle him until he is sorry he did not shoot himself in the head, for she dotes on him and always has."

"Fool fell off his horse," Lord Wyndham ground out.

Demi bit her lip. "I feel awful that I didn't warn you it wasn't at all safe to go off with him. Only two years ago, he shot his groundskeeper in the ... uh ... seat of his breeches."

Lord Wyndham's lips curled in a smile. "I am far more fortunate than I thought."

To her relief, the surgeon arrived. She got to her feet, relinquishing Lord Wyndham's hand with reluctance and moved away from the bed. "I think I'll go and sit in the garden for a little while. If you need anything...."

The manservant gave her an approving look and escorted her to the door. Demi stared at the door panel for a moment after it closed behind her and finally turned and fled from the Abbey to pace the garden. As badly as she'd wanted to stay with him, she knew very well that it would not have been allowed, and, in any case, she didn't want to increase his discomfort by witnessing his suffering when he preferred that she didn't.

It was some comfort that the wound was in his calf-- not much, but a little bit. It also made her feel a little better that the manservant seemed to think his boot had protected him somewhat and that no major vein had been damaged. She didn't think he would have told her that if it hadn't been true.

Infection was always a danger, however, and until the surgeon checked, they couldn't know for certain just how much damage there was.

Finally, worn out from pacing and worry, Demi sat on the bench she'd occupied earlier and stared into the distance, replaying the few memories she had between them over and over and wondering morosely if that was all she'd ever have ... a handful of memories. The sun had almost dropped behind the trees by the time Lord Wyndham's manservant came out to find her.

She looked up at him, trying to keep the fear out of her expression.

"The surgeon seems to consider that there will be no

lasting damage and that his lordship should be on the road to a speedy recovery now that he's removed the lead and cleaned the wounds."

Demi was so relieved she covered her face with her hands and burst into tears. Embarrassed by her lack of restraint, she did her best to choke them back. "I'm … so relieved. Thank you for taking the time to come and tell me…."

"Fitzhugh, Miss. The surgeon gave him something to help him rest."

Demi nodded, then sniffed, mopping the tears from her face with her hand. "You will let me know if he needs … anything?"

"Certainly, Miss. I'll keep you informed."

When he'd gone, she composed herself and went upstairs to bathe and dress for dinner. Phoebe and her Aunt were in the parlor when she came down again, both of them looking uncharacteristically subdued.

"How is Geoffrey?" she asked when she'd taken a seat.

Alma Moreland blinked, as if coming out of a trance and stared at her for several moments. "Well enough. He has a very badly sprained ankle. The surgeon secmed to think he might lose a part of his finger, but he sewed it up and said we could wait and see if it healed properly before there was any talk of removing it."

Demi nodded, but as awful as the thought was that Geoffrey might lose his finger, it paled beside the possibility that Lord Wyndham stood an equal chance of losing all or part of his leg if the wound became infected, and possibly his life. "Did he tell you what happened?"

She sighed. "They were all near hysterical over the incident. Not one of them had a very clear idea. Apparently, Geoffrey lost his seat and somehow managed to discharge his gun as he fell. We will be ruined if Lord Wyndham dies on us."

What little sympathy Demi had felt toward her aunt vanished at that remark. It was just like her only to see her own side of the situation.

She supposed it was understandable to an extent. It was only natural to feel more concern over her own family. But what of Lord Wyndham's family? And what of Lord Wyndham himself, if he survived but lost his leg? She'd not even so much as mentioned any sort of anxiety over his injury.

She discovered when dinner was announced that Geoffrey's friends, fearful no doubt that their friend had killed a peer of the realm, had decamped almost as soon as they'd dropped Geoffrey and Lord Wyndham at the Abbey. Lady Moreland had shuttled Phoebe's visitors off when she'd come down from overseeing the physician that had been sent for to attend to Geoffrey. Reverend Flemming called just as they settled in the dining room, but to Demi's surprise, Lady Moreland sent word that they were not receiving visitors due to the invalids upstairs. And so it was only Demi, her cousin Phoebe, and her aunt who dined together that evening, none of whom were disposed to conversation.

When they'd finished, Alma Moreland retired to her son's room to 'cheer' the invalid, Phoebe vanished upstairs behind her and Demi was left to entertain herself as she would. She sent for Sarah to find out if a tray had been sent up for Lord Wyndham. Sarah assured her that the cook had prepared a tray for him exactly to the doctor's specifications and sent it up some time ago and that Lord Wyndham had dutifully, though not very happily, consumed the beef broth he needed to help rebuild his blood. Demi was a little doubtful. It sounded like very little for so large a man, but Sarah seemed to think it was just the thing he needed.

"His manservant, Fitzhugh, is attending him?"

Sarah nodded. "He seems a very efficient sort. It was a fortunate circumstance that Lord Wyndham had arranged for Fitzhugh to deliver their luncheon to them on the shoot. If he had not been there with the carriage they would have had to send to the Abbey for one to carry Lord Wyndham. His lordship's horse caught more of the blast than him and had to be put down, not that his lordship was in any shape to be ridin' a horse after that anyway."

"I don't suppose Mr. Fitzhugh needs anyone to help-- perhaps to stay with Lord Wyndham and give him time to rest?"

Sarah smiled. "I already offered, Miss. He was none too happy about it, but the doctor said his lordship was not to be left alone for more than a few minutes for the next several days...until he's certain his lordship is out of the woods, so he accepted my offer. His lordship's got a touch of fever, but the doctor seemed to think that was to be expected. He left medicine for the fever. Yer not to worry about it. We'll watch over Lord Wyndham and make sure he's right as rain before you know it."

"I could stay with him part of the time, too."

"Now, Miss Demitria, you know your aunt would have apoplexy! A young lady has no place in a gentleman's bedchamber."

Demi sighed irritably. "You must know I've no reputation to worry about any longer. Horatia Wynthrope was here, for heaven's sake! If it had been anyone but her! But Aunt Alma has sent her home and you may be certain there will not be anyone in the ton who does not know of my disgrace by tomorrow."

Sarah's jaw set. "As unhappy as it is that ye'll have to marry the man that ruined ye, yer not the first and ye'll not be the last to find herself in that position. There's naught in that little incident that the marriage won't fix. Being in a man's room that's neither yer fiancé nor yer husband is another matter altogether."

Demi wasn't satisfied, but decided to let it go, for the moment, at least. So long as Lord Wyndham didn't worsen, she was willing to contain herself and stay out of the sick room. If his conditioned worsened, however, she fully intended to help, regardless of what anyone had to say about it.

She certainly didn't care about protecting her reputation for Jonathan Flemming, not when she knew very well that he had premeditatedly ruined her to begin with to make certain she could not back out of the engagement. She wouldn't have been surprised in the least to discover his intention had been to get her with child if possible to insure his hold on her. He had not needed to go so far as that. Her disheveled appearance had been enough to imply it, but despite the fact that she'd been very agitated at the time, she was certain he had not needed to throw her down on the seat of the carriage only to steal a few kisses. He'd had his knee between her thighs and her skirts halfway up her legs when she'd managed to kick the hand brake free the last time and he might well have made a third attempt if she hadn't had the good sense to wound his little pet by grinding her knee into it.

She supposed it was possible that he had only intended to steal a few kisses and had lost control, but he did not strike her as a man who had difficulty controlling himself in general. He seemed far more cold and calculating than impulsive.

It occurred to her to wonder if he would even care if her reputation was further sullied. She doubted it, whatever anyone else might think about it. She didn't doubt, however, that he would make her rue the day she'd cuckolded him. She was as certain of that as she was that she would not let it weigh with her if it transpired that Lord Wyndham had need of her.

Chapter Seven

As tired as she was from the anxiety that had plagued her since Lord Wyndham's accident, Demi found she could only sleep fitfully. She drowsed, but she did not sleep so deeply that she failed to notice the increase in activity at Lord Wyndham's door late in the night, despite the fact that his room was two doors down from hers and nearer the stairs.

Climbing from the bed, she grabbed a robe and slipped into it, securing it by the ribbon beneath her breasts, then crept to the door and opened it wide enough that she could look down the hall. Sarah, she saw, was carrying a pail of water into the invalid's room. Demi's heart lurched. That could only mean that his fever had risen.

Glancing up and down the hall to make certain no one else was around, Demi dashed for the door to Lord Wyndham's room and tested the knob. Finding that it was not locked, she went in, closing the door behind her. Her gaze went toward the bed first where she saw that he was moving restlessly, his complexion as flushed now as it had been pale before. Sarah was in the act of pouring water into the basin. She glanced around when she'd filled it, stopping dead in her tracks when she saw Demitria.

Frowning, she moved to the table beside the bed and set the basin down, then turned and made a shooing motion in Demi's direction. Demi ignored her, instead moving to stand near the foot of the bed. "He's worse, isn't he?"

Placing a finger to her lips, Sarah rounded the bed, caught her arm and escorted her to the door. "His fevers up a bit, that's all. The medicine the doctor left's helping, but Mr. Fitzhugh said if he got too hot to bathe him with cool water."

"I'll do it."

"Ye will not!" Sarah whispered in outrage. "I'll not be

leavin' ye in here in his lordship's room in nothing but yer night rail!"

Demi's eyes narrowed. "How long have you been in here?"

Sarah looked taken aback. "Since around eleven, but that's got nothing to do with this."

"You're tired. What if you fall asleep? I've slept for hours. I can do it ... and everyone else is asleep. No one will know the difference."

"Have you ever attended a sick room?"

Demi gave her a look. "You know very well I haven't."

"Well, there you are."

"How much experience can it take to bathe someone with cold water? Just tell me what to do."

"Ye'll go back to your room, Miss, before your aunt discovers ye here or I'll tell her myself!"

Demi's lips tightened. "Tell her. I'm staying. You can go get some sleep and come back before anyone wakes up and I'll leave and no one will be the wiser. Or you can run tell my aunt right now and have the whole household up, in which case everybody will know I've been in his room all this time, in my nightgown, and they can speculate about what I've been doing all they want."

Sarah released an angry breath. "You'll not give me any trouble about leaving when I get back?"

Demi shook her head and after giving her a disgusted look, Sarah led her back to the side of the bed and explained the procedure for cooling the fever. She stayed long enough to watch Demi for a few moments to make certain she was doing as she'd been told and finally left. When Demi dipped the cloth the second time, wrung it out and turned back to him, she discovered that he was looking at her. She smiled, not certain of whether he was actually aware of her or not. A faint smile curled his lips and he closed his eyes once more as she carefully placed the cloth over his forehead.

"You should not have come, Demi," he murmured a little hoarsely.

"I won't stay long. I promise."

"At all."

"Are you thirsty?" she asked, changing the subject. He nodded and she dropped the cloth in the washbasin and went to get him a glass of water. He struggled up on one elbow when she returned with the glass of water, wincing as pain shot through his leg. "You should have let me help you," she admonished, slipping an arm around him to help steady him while he drank. When he'd drained the glass, he asked for another and Demi hurried across the room again, bringing the pitcher with her that time. Finally satisfied, he lay back again and closed his eyes.

Demi touched the back of her fingers to his cheeks and then lay her hand across his forehead to check the warmth. Before she could pull her hand away, he reached up and placed his own over it. "Your hand feels so cool. I'm damnably hot in this nightshirt."

"You're liable to catch your ... a chill without it," she amended.

He opened one eye and looked at her. "I'm not likely to die of so paltry a wound ... unless it gets infected, of course. I've had worse."

Gently disengaging her hand from his, she wrung the cloth out and placed it on his forehead again. "We won't let that happen," she said after a moment.

"We?"

"Mr. Fitzhugh, Sarah and I--we'll take good care of you. You'll see. You'll probably be feeling much better by tomorrow and tired of lying in bed."

"I'm tired of that now. How long have I been here?"

Demi bit her lip, feeling a flutter of alarm that he'd lost track of the time. She could not think that that was a good sign. "Since about noon today ... well, I suppose yesterday now."

He frowned as she removed cloth and dipped it into the water again. When she turned back, she discovered he was studying her. "Flemming should have been horse whipped. I'd have had a better opinion of Lord Moreland if he'd at least offered to instead of sitting there with his mouth agape like a fish out of water."

Demi flushed uncomfortably at the reminder of her fall from grace, but at that last comment, she looked at him in surprise. "He's only a boy, and not even half the size of Mr. Flemming."

"He's as much a man as he'll ever be, I'll warrant. He should have called him out."

Demi gave him a look. "I can't imagine getting himself killed would've helped me in the least. You know how bad he is with a gun. He could not hit the side of a barn if he was standing no more than ten paces from it."

"He hit me--without even trying I might add."

"Exactly. If he'd been trying, most likely he would've hit one of the others."

He chuckled, then winced as the movement jarred his injured leg.

Demi frowned. "Sarah said I could give you a few drops of laudanum for the pain if you needed it," she said tentatively.

He shook his head. "I'd as soon keep my wits about me."

"Sleep is what you need to mend," she said admonishingly. "I didn't intend to wake you, or to keep you awake."

"You are a font of wisdom for one so young," he murmured, smiling without opening his eyes. "Where did you learn that?"

Demi frowned, trying to think. "My mother," she said finally, with a touch of surprise.

He looked up at her. "You don't remember much about your parents, do you? I've never heard you mention them before."

The comment struck her as odd, since she'd only spoken to him a handful of times in all the time she'd known him. She dismissed it finally, shaking her head. "Not much. I was very little when they were killed."

He frowned. "You were eight when you came to live with the Morelands."

She looked at him in surprise. "Did I tell you that? I guess I must have. Almost eight, anyway."

"Surely that's old enough you should remember a great deal?"

She concentrated on rinsing the cloth again. Discovering that the water was warm, she got up and poured the water from the bowl into the chamber pot, then refilled it from the bucket Sarah had left. Lord Wyndham was studying her when she returned. She glanced at him a couple of times as she soaked the cloth and finally sighed. "There's nothing wrong with me. I just don't remember very much. I'm sure there are probably plenty of people who don't remember their childhood that well."

"In truth, you're little more than that now," he said wryly.

She sent him an irritated look. "Geoffrey is only a little older than me and you said he was a man. If that is true, then I am most definitely a woman, not a child."

Something gleamed in his eyes. A slow smile curled his lips. "Prove it."

Demi's stomach went weightless at the look on his face, but she couldn't help but chuckle. Leaning down until her lips hovered just above his, she whispered, "When you're better."

"Tease," he said without heat when she pulled away.

"And you're not?" Her back and shoulders had already begun to burn from bending over to apply the cool cloth. When she'd dipped it and wrung it out again, she sat on the edge of the bed.

"No. I always keep my promises."

It was on the tip of her tongue to remind him that he'd been the one to call a halt to their interlude in the meadow, but she thought it best not to. The entire conversation was wildly inappropriate. She doubted, if her situation had been different, that he would have spoken so outrageously. She couldn't imagine that he would speak so suggestively to Phoebe--or any other lady for that matter--but then a lady would not have been in his room in the dead of night, wearing nothing but her nightgown. A lady would not have allowed, much less encouraged, the kisses they'd shared.

She'd always believed she was a lady. Now she wondered if she never had been, or if it was only that being around Lord Wyndham was enough to completely undermine the fragile foundation of her upbringing.

Undoubtedly it was, for she found that, instead of being shocked or outraged as she should have been, she *wanted* to prove it. She wanted to experience everything the words implied.

If only she dared!

She managed a smile. "I'm glad you're feeling well enough to … have such things on your mind, at least."

"I would have to be on my deathbed not to have such things on my mind with you in my bed … wearing nothing but your nightgown."

Demi blushed and would've sprang up from the bed except that he'd undoubtedly expected it. He dropped one arm across her lap, curling his hand along her hip. His grip was surprisingly strong for someone supposedly weakened by fever and injury. She relaxed, unwilling to risk jarring his leg and causing him any more pain. "My lord…."

"Garrett."

"It wouldn't be prop--" She cut herself off, realizing how absurd it was to prose on about the impropriety of calling him by his Christian name under the circumstances. She shook her head at him. "You should try to rest, Garrett. If Sarah finds you awake when she comes back, she'll accuse me of not taking proper care of you and she won't let me come back."

"Lie with me then."

Demi's eyes widened. "Are you mad! What if someone were to come in?"

He shrugged. "Lock the door."

Blood surged into her cheeks. "I couldn't do that! It'd be worse if the door was locked."

"It'll be worse if your aunt decides to drop in to check on me and finds you here."

Demi's eyes widened. She honestly hadn't thought of that. She frowned, wondering if there was any real danger of it and realized that it wasn't beyond the realms of possibility. If her aunt woke and decided to check on her son, she might also decide to check on Lord Wyndham. "You are a very bad influence on me," she chided him. "I'll lock the door, but only because I don't want to take a chance on Aunt Alma finding me in here. I'm not getting into bed with you!"

He said nothing and after a moment, she got up and moved across the room, locking the door. When she returned, she took the cloth from his head and dipped it into the basin once more. She'd just twisted it to wring the water from it, when he wrapped an arm around her waist and pulled her back, rolling to his side and depositing her on the bed beside him. She gasped in surprise, but froze when he let out a sharp gasp of pain. She sat up. "You've hurt your leg!"

Scrambling over the mattress, she pulled the coverlet back to check his bandages. To her relief, she saw no sign of fresh bleeding. Covering his leg carefully once more, she turned to look at him. "You shouldn't have done that."

He dropped an arm across his eyes. "Probably not. It hurts like hell now."

Demi sighed. "Sarah was right. I shouldn't have come."

"Sarah was … but I'm glad you ignored her."

Scooting up the bed, she pulled his arm away from his face and checked his forehead. It was still very warm, but it had cooled a good bit from before. Instead of laying the cloth across his forehead, she gently wiped his face. "I'll get you some laudanum."

He took the cloth from her hand and tossed it in the general direction of the basin. It hit the edge and slid in. Turning back to her, he pulled her down and tucked her against his side. "You rest. You need it more than I do."

She didn't resist, but not altogether because she was afraid of hurting him again, or making him hurt himself. "You said you'd rest if I would lie beside you."

"I had something else in mind, actually."

Demi smiled faintly. "I know."

Slipping an arm behind her back, he caught her arm and draped it across his chest, then leaned down and kissed the tip of her nose. "Keep in mind that this is a temporary set back."

Chapter Eight

Despite the comment, Lord Wyndham was far worse the following day. Demi didn't dare even approach the door after the fuss Sarah put up when she returned and discovered the door to the room locked. She had seemed slightly mollified when Demi had pointed out that she'd thought it best, in case her aunt woke, but she was still deeply suspicious and made no attempt to hide it.

The surgeon was summoned again the following afternoon. He lanced the wound, which was showing some signs of trying to become infected, advised Fitzhugh to clean the wound and change the dressings every eight hours or so, and left again, shaking his head. Demi was beside herself with worry. She spent most of the day in the library with a book open in her lap, listening to the footsteps in the room overhead and trying to interpret the meaning. She managed to waylay Sarah at one point, but the news did nothing to comfort her. "He's a bit out of his head. Could be the laudanum--the doctor gave him a right smart dose of that when he bled him--but it don't seem to me that the medicine for his fever's doin' a lot of good. He's been askin' for a solicitor for hours. Mr. Fitzhugh told me to send a boy round to fetch one for him ... thought it might quiet him down."

Demi thought for several moments that she might faint. Sarah, looking more than a little alarmed, caught her arms, dragged her back into the library and made her sit down. "Here now! We can't be havin' none of this, Miss. Ye know what'll be goin' through everybody's mind if ye faint and I have to run for smellin' salts!"

Demi nodded numbly, but she didn't really care what they thought anymore. "I'm fine. Go. See to ... your errand."

"Yer sure?"

She nodded again. She spent the rest of the day wallowing in regrets, wishing she'd done any number of things differently. Her deepest regrets though, were that she'd not somehow prevented Garrett from going with her cousin on the shoot; that she'd allowed herself to be bullied into going off with Mr. Flemming when she might otherwise have known about Geoffrey's plans; and that she'd allowed propriety, and her fear of what other people would think of her, to prevent her from grabbing what she could of happiness while she could.

She tried *not* to think about the possibility that Garrett wouldn't recover, but she spent most of the remainder of the day praying for another chance. If she just had one more opportunity, she would seize it, take what happiness she could and worry about the consequences later. There would be plenty of time for regrets afterward, she knew, but at least she wouldn't have to regret what she'd missed out on.

As interminable as the day was, the night was worse. Exhausted emotionally, she fell asleep almost as soon as she climbed into her bed, but she'd been lying awake for an hour or more when the tap came on her door. Throwing the covers off, Demi rushed hopefully across the room and snatched the door open. To her surprise, instead of Sarah, Mr. Fitzhugh was standing just outside. "His lordship's been asking for you all day, Miss Standish," he said in a hushed whisper.

"A moment," she whispered back and rushed to grab her robe from the foot of her bed.

Sarah, she discovered, was in Garrett's room, methodically rinsing the cloth, wringing it out and placing it across his forehead. Leaving it for only a few moments, she started the process all over again. She looked across the room finally at Demi, who'd stopped just inside the door.

Nodding, she dropped the cloth on the table and went to pour the water out and replace it with cooler water. When she'd carried the basin back to the bed, she placed the cooled cloth on his head once more, then turned and headed for the door.

The click of the door closing jolted Demi out of her

frozen fear and she moved to the side of the bed to take Sarah's place. He'd dragged the cloth from his forehead, she saw. When she reached to take it from his hand, he grasped her wrist painfully. Startled, she glanced at his face quickly. His eyes were open, but she could see no recognition in them. Lifting her free hand, she stroked his cheek, resisting the urge to burst into tears. "Garrett?"

Something flickered in his eyes. Slowly, his grip on her wrist loosened. "Demi?"

Her chin wobbled so badly it took her several moments to speak. "Yes."

He frowned, obviously trying to gather his thoughts. "Made arrangements," he managed finally.

Demi lost control then. Bursting into sobs, she threw herself on his chest. "Don't talk like that! Don't even think it! It's bad luck."

"Shhh. Can't afford not to. My position. People depend on me. Give you my word I don't expect the worst."

Demi choked back her sobs and sat back, sniffing. "You don't?"

He dragged in a ragged breath and shook his head slightly. "I have responsibilities. Can't afford to ignore the possibility of disaster. Made arrangements for you. If anything happens, Fitzhugh will explain."

Demi mopped the tears from her cheeks and studied him in confusion. She could tell, however, that his throat was parched with thirst. His voice was rough with it. Getting up, she retrieved the pitcher and glass and helped him to drink until he indicated that he'd had enough.

He seemed to drift off again when he lay back, but he didn't seem as restless as before.

She tested his forehead and cheeks, but if his fever had abated at all, she couldn't tell it.

She stayed, as she had the night before until Sarah came and shooed her away.

Despite her anxieties, she'd had several nights of little or no sleep and when she fell into her bed, she slept the sleep of the truly exhausted and didn't waken until nearly noon the following day. "Reverend Flemming has called again," Sarah announced tightly when she arrived in Demi's room to help her dress. "Lady Moreland invited him to stay for luncheon."

Demi's belly immediately clenched with dismay, but she dismissed it. "How is Lord Wyndham?"

Sarah shook her head. "I can't tell he's a whit better, but he seems no worse. The doctor dropped by earlier ... said his lordship'd reach his crisis today. Either the fever'll break, or...."

Demi nodded, fighting the urge to burst into tears. It wouldn't do to arrive downstairs in a state of utter turmoil. She knew better than to think she would be allowed to stay in her room and ignore Mr. Flemming's visit.

When she arrived downstairs, she discovered Geoffrey ensconced in the parlor, his leg propped on a stool and a mound of pillows. His expression was a curious mixture of the sullen schoolboy and repentant transgressor. Reverend Flemming was sitting on one side of him and his mother the other, both, apparently, lecturing him on his recent exploits. Phoebe, seated on the couch opposite the threesome, was wearing the smug look of the pious.

Demi was of more than half a mind to simply turn around and retreat. The look of entreaty Geoffrey sent her way stopped her. She was angry with him for hurting Garrett, but she knew it hadn't been intentional and there seemed little point in heaping her disapproval on top of that already weighing his shoulders down.

Sighing, she moved into the parlor, looked around, and finally took a seat in a chair that sat alone, at some distance from the others. If she thought Flemming would take it as the rejection it was, she was wrong. He got up at once, smiling as if his welcome was assured, and dragged a chair over next to hers.

Demi gave him an unwelcoming glare.

His brows rose. He possessed himself of one of her hands after a short wrestle for it. "I only came to apologize for my unconscionable behavior the other day."

She sent him a look. She didn't believe a word it and she took no pains to hide her doubt.

He frowned. "You are very sheltered, and a properly brought up young lady. You would know nothing about the baser instincts of men. I lost my head."

Demi's eyes narrowed. "You would have lost it from your shoulders if I'd had anything to remove it with."

Both Geoffrey and Phoebe snickered and Flemming reddened alarmingly. Before he could think up a response, however, the butler announced luncheon. Demi jumped up at once, trying to tug her hand free. Flemming's tightened on hers until she winced and ceased tugging. He smiled then. "I'd far rather escort you in to dine, but our invalid needs some assistance," he said coolly, releasing her hand finally.

Demi fumed, massaging her hand and staring daggers at his back, but finally turned and followed Phoebe into the small dining parlor. They dined in virtual silence. Alma Moreland made some attempt to carry on a civilized conversation and was supported by the Reverend Flemming, but neither Geoffrey nor Phoebe seemed inclined to contribute more than a comment or two and Demi refused to be drawn into the conversation at all.

She would have risen and left immediately after they'd finished, but Flemming forestalled, her, tucking her hand beneath his arm and escorting her back to the parlor. When everyone was settled in the parlor once more, he stood and looked them all over as if he was about to begin a sermon and wanted to make certain he had everyone's attention. "I have posted the banns."

Demi stared at him, too stunned even to speak for several moments. No one else seemed to have a problem, however. Phoebe uttered, "But I thought--"

Her mother cut her off. "But this is delightful news! Very good thinking on your part, Mr. Flemming! This should still the wagging tongues quickly enough."

Demi found her voice. She jumped to her feet. "You can *un*post them! I *told* you I would not marry you, not under any circumstances whatsoever!"

Her aunt gave her a stern look. "Nonsense! Of course you will. You accepted, the banns have been posted. Your disgraceful behavior the other day aside, you would be ruined if you even considered such a thing!"

"*My* disgraceful behavior!" Demi gasped in outrage. "How *dare* you blame that on me!"

"You forget yourself," Alma Moreland snapped furiously. "I should have known nothing I could do would cure you of your father's wildness! Or your mother's utter lack of good sense, for that matter."

Instead of being cowed by her aunt's wrath, Demi's eyes narrowed. "I'm curious to know why you're so obsessed by my father's behavior," she said tightly.

To her surprise, Alma Moreland turned as white as a sheet before reddening almost to the hue of a plum. "Nonsense!" she snapped, avoiding Demi's gaze. "If by obsessed you mean dealing with his difficult offspring, then I suppose you might call it so."

At that moment, everything became crystal clear to Demi. Alma Moreland *was* obsessed with her father. She'd been in love with him when he'd run off with her mother and she'd hated both of them ever since ... still hated them. Her marriage to a man of wealth and title hadn't bothered either one of them. They'd been happy and in love and couldn't have cared less that they lived from hand to mouth, so long as they were together. *She* had been Alma Moreland's chance to get even.

"He's dead. Mother's dead and you're not going to make me pay for what you think they did to you."

Alma Moreland glared at her with pure hatred for a split second before she very carefully composed her features. "You're delusional. Go to your room and consider very carefully before you think to throw away Mr. Flemming's offer. I'm surprised he will even consider going forward with the agreement, but he is a good man and willing to overlook the folly of youth."

Whirling angrily, Demi stalked from the room.

"She needs a firm hand," her aunt said as she left.

"I believe I am up to the challenge," Jonathan Flemming responded coolly.

A maid was sent up to inform her that she was to be confined to her room until she was ready to 'behave properly'. She took that to mean until she agreed with her aunt's plans for her. She wouldn't have cared except that she couldn't bear to be locked away so that she couldn't even find out how Lord Wyndham was faring.

Her aunt, apparently believing she might try to flee, had stationed a rotation of 'guards' to patrol the upper hall. Even Sarah was forbidden to come to her room.

She would've immediately capitulated, just to have a chance to see Garrett, but she knew her aunt wouldn't believe it even if she tried. She would have to endure several days of punishment at least before her aunt believed her properly repentant.

She would go crazy worrying about Garrett.

It was well past midnight when Demi heard someone pause briefly outside her door and a faint slithering noise. At first, she thought it must be her aunt, listening to make certain she was still in her room, but then she noticed a piece of paper on the floor. Leaping from the bed, she rushed over to pick it up.

Her hands were shaking so badly she had difficulty lighting the lamp, but the moonlight streaming through her windows wasn't bright enough to read the note. The handwriting was unfamiliar, but perfectly formed and very precise.

His fever has broken. He is on the mend.

She was still clutching the note to her chest when the door opened abruptly. Demi took one glance at the look on her aunt's face and dropped the note into the lamp. The light blazed briefly as the note blackened, curled and then disintegrated.

Her aunt's lips tightened. After a moment, she left without a word, slamming the door behind her.

Demi let out the breath she hadn't even known she was holding and climbed back into her bed. Relief, so profound it brought tears to her eyes, swept over her, and gratitude--both for the fact that Garrett was recovering, and for her unknown benefactor who'd gone to such trouble to let her know. She suspected it had been Mr. Fitzhugh who'd written the note. Sarah couldn't read or write, but very likely it had been she who'd slipped the note beneath the door.

She was certain the effort would cost her, but it had been well worth it and was deeply appreciated regardless of what her aunt might decide to do in retaliation.

She just hoped Sarah didn't get into trouble.

A pounding at her window the following morning woke her to her aunt's retaliation. Crawling from the bed, Demi staggered to the window and pulled the curtain back. One of the yardmen was hammering on the edge of her window sill. She stared at him in confusion, still too sleepy, at first, to comprehend what he was doing standing on a ladder outside her room. Noticing her at last, he paused in his task, looked to his right, then left and finally twisted around and looked behind him.

Curious, Demi leaned toward the window and looked around, as well. She didn't see anyone, which was no great surprise since it was barely daybreak, but apparently that was what he'd been trying to determine. Shoving his hammer into a loop on his belt, he grasped the edge of the window and pushed it up while Demi stared at him, completely baffled now. If he hadn't been nailing her window closed, what had he been doing with the hammer?

Pulling a pouch from his belt, he held it out to her. "Sarah says, bread and water for three days. This should tide you over."

Demi took the pouch and opened it, staring down at the assortment of fruit and cheese.

"Stash it where your aunt can't find it."

He closed the window then, hammered a few more times on the sill, climbed down the ladder ... and walked off, leaving the ladder under the window.

Demi bit her lip. Half the servants on the staff were going to be dismissed before this was over. It was heart warming, though, to realize someone was on her side.

Sighing, she drew the drapes across the window once more, found a place at the bottom of her armoire in a hat box to hide her stash of food and climbed back into the bed. There was little to do locked in her room all day beyond sleep, and she'd had so little in so long that it was no great feat to go back to sleep once more.

The three days she remained locked in her room ranked among the worst in her life. On the fourth day, a seamstress arrived with two assistants to take her measurements for her wedding gown and make the final fittings. Demi made a supreme effort to behave as if she was completely subdued. It wasn't as difficult as it might have been otherwise, for the days she'd spent locked in her room had severely lowered her spirits.

She was rewarded for her 'good' behavior by being allowed to join the family downstairs for dinner. Unfortunately, the 'family' included Jonathan Flemming and merely seeing him was sufficient to set her temper at a slow boil. It took far more of an effort to behave civilly toward him even than it did her aunt. Alma Moreland, by and large, ignored her. Jonathan Flemming was determined to draw her into conversation.

However, now that Garrett was on the mend, she knew he would be leaving soon. If she did not convince her aunt and Mr. Flemming that she was meek and compliant, she would not get the chance to see him before he left the Abbey.

It still took more of an effort than she would ever have thought possible, particularly since she had to endure an evening in the parlor afterward. Finally, however, he took his leave. Shortly after that, she went up to her room to get ready for bed.

For the first time in nearly a week, Sarah was allowed to come in to help her prepare for bed. "How is Gar-- Lord Wyndham faring?" she asked the moment the door closed behind her maid.

Sarah rolled her eyes. "He has the devil of a temper when he's crossed. Mending far too slow to suit him. Ready to shake the dust of Moreland Abbey, no doubt about that."

"Well enough to receive visitors?" Demi asked in a hopeful whisper.

Sarah eyed her with disfavor. "Don't be gettin' wild ideas now, Miss. He's well enough he's no need to be watched round the clock and Mr. Fitzhugh is handling things just fine. Yer not needed in the sick room, and unless ye want to be locked up in here till yer wedding day, ye'll take my advice and stay put."

Demi studied her maid speculatively. "We're very much of a size."

"Aye. The gowns ye've give me only needed a nip here an' a tuck there ... *No*! Absolutely not! Lady

Moreland would have my head."

Chapter Nine

Sarah was a bit more buxom, and a few inches taller than Demi, and she was more inclined to think the gowns, especially since they'd originally belonged to Phoebe, had needed no nips or tucks, but she wasn't about to quibble over it. It took her night twenty minutes to talk Sarah into the scheme and she was still far from happy about it when she climbed into Demi's bed and pulled the covers over her head.

Demi moved to the mirror to check her appearance, front and back, and decided she was satisfied. She might not pass for Sarah in any room bright enough to distinguish her features, but there would be no bright rooms that she would have to pass through at this hour of the night.

Her hair was a few shades darker than Sarah's, who was more nearly blonde than brunette, but the mob cap her aunt required the servants to wear covered that discrepancy rather nicely.

Mr. Fitzhugh was the only hurtle she would have to overcome.

Dousing the lamps in the room, she waited until her eyes had adjusted to the moonlight filtering into the room, then moved across to the door and eased it open. A couple of servants were standing near the head of the stairs, talking--the changing of the guard--but as she'd expected, there was only one lamp lit in the upper hall. Bundling the clothes she'd been wearing into a tight ball, she drew in a deep sustaining breath and closed the door softly behind her and headed for Lord Wyndham's room and tapped on the door. Fitzhugh, who'd apparently been on the point of leaving, opened it almost instantly.

He was holding a lamp, but since it was higher than her head, she thought it probably cast her face in shadow. She bobbed her head. "I just thought I'd see if his lordship had laundry needed takin' down," she whispered, trying to mimic Sarah's speech patterns and accent.

Fitzhugh hesitated. "I was on the point of retiring and thought I'd take the laundry down myself."

Demi shrugged. "There's no point in us both goin'."

Fitzhugh glanced behind him but finally looked at her again and nodded. "Thank you, Sarah. I left them by the chair." With that, he stepped back, allowing her to enter, then proceeded through the door, closing it softly behind him.

Sarah breathed a sigh of relief when he'd gone, and glanced around the room. A single lamp had been left lit on the table near the door. It had been dimmed, but allowed enough light for her to make out the furnishings well enough to keep from running into them. Garrett was sprawled in the bed, bare to the waist, apparently sleeping soundly, and a ripple of doubt went through her. She hadn't really considered anything beyond getting into the room. She supposed she had assumed that he would be awake as he had been before. Disappointment filled her. She didn't want to wake him when he'd been ill so long.

She had only told Sarah that she wished to see him, however. Moreover, if the servants in the hallway had overheard her conversation, they would expect her to merely collect the bundle of laundry and depart.

Mentally shrugging, she looked around for the laundry. There were two high backed, overstuffed easy chairs near the hearth, but no sign of clothing in or around them. Deciding he must have meant the chair near the bed, she set the bundle she was carrying down, tiptoed cautiously across the room, and peered at the chair. It was far darker than she'd expected, but she thought she discerned darker shapes among the shadows. In any case, the chair near the bed was the only other chair in the room.

Moving quietly to keep from disturbing him, she leaned down and checked the seat of the chair with her hand. Encountering nothing, she moved a little closer and bent over again, feeling around on the floor. Her questing fingers brushed fabric that time. Grasping it, she lifted it and dropped it in the seat of the chair, then felt around until she thought she'd found everything. She'd no sooner finished piling the clothing than they tipped and slid off the other side of the chair. Repressing an exclamation of irritation, she moved around to the front of the chair and reached for the clothes that had fallen off the other side.

She didn't notice the slight breeze that wafted across her knees.

The hand that settled on her buttocks beneath her skirts brought her jackknifing upright.

Twisting around, she discovered Lord Wyndham was leaning over the side of the bed, her skirts over his head. "G--my lord!" she gasped in a sharp whisper, snatching her skirts down.

Instead of releasing her, his hand snaked around her waist, pulling her back. "You shouldn't entice a man with such temptation if you're of no mind to share," he murmured huskily.

There was repressed laughter in his voice, but there was no doubting that he was completely serious, particularly since he nuzzled his face in the cleft of her buttocks. Even through her clothing she could feel the heat of his breath and the imprint of his face against her lower cheeks and it sent a jittery sort of twang along her nerve endings. Horrified, she shoved at the hand he'd wrapped around her hips. Obligingly, he withdrew his arm a little way, then slid his hand downward, slipping it between her thighs and cupping her femininity.

Demi's heart seemed to stop in her chest for several moments, then launched into a full out gallop, making it difficult to drag in a decent breath of air. She thought for several moments that she might faint.

"M-my lord!" she gasped finally.

"You wouldn't deprive a starving man, would you?"

He thought she was one of the maids, she realized abruptly. He was suggesting ... she allow him to toss her skirts up. A barrage of conflicting emotions pelted her on that instant, jealousy foremost among them--hurt and anger. It wiped out much of the heated desire coursing through her at his intimate touch, not all of it, but enough that she could think more rationally.

He would not have touched her so familiarly, she

knew, if he'd realized who she was.

She slipped her hand down over his, the one he'd pushed between her thighs--to pull him away, she was--almost--certain. His fingers discovered the opening in her pantalets at that moment, however, and one long finger stroked along the seam of her nether lips. She froze, her breath caught in her throat as a dizzying rush of unfamiliar sensations washed through her.

He didn't know her. It was too dark in the room for him to recognize her. She could allow him to do anything and he would never know. No one would ever know. It could be her secret joy, that she'd given herself to the man she loved before she had to receive the man she hated.

It was a wonderful, terrifying, thought.

But he'd been near death only a few days earlier. Was he really up to something like this? And even if he thought he was, should he?

She licked her lips. "You'll…." She paused, cleared her throat. "Ye'll hurt yer leg, yer lordship. Yer not a well man."

He removed the hand that had been gently exploring her. She thought he meant to release her. Instead, he tugged her around, caught her waist and dragged her across him, depositing her on the bed on her back on the other side of him. Before she could do more than gasp in surprise, he covered her mouth with his own.

He kissed her as if he was indeed starving, as if he would consume her. The moment his mouth opened over hers, such heat swept through her that it washed the last of her doubts before it. She slipped her hand along his shoulder and threaded her fingers in his dark, unbound hair, cupping the back of his head as he possessed her mouth with hungry urgency. He cupped one hand along her face, his fingers splayed. Slowly, as his tongue raked along hers in an intimate dance that generated waves of heat between them, he skated his hand downward, delved beneath the neckline of her gown and scooped her breast from beneath the fabric.

A cool breath of air wafted across her bare breast, and she felt the skin tighten as her nipple hardened, blood surging into the sensitive tip as he flicked the hardened bud it had become with one finger. Her belly clenched. A wash of warmth and moisture gathered in her femininity. She shifted beneath him in discomfort, uncertain of the strange uneasiness that assailed her. She forgot all about trying to analyze it, however, when he broke the kiss and replaced his finger with his mouth on her breast. A hard shock of sensation struck her the moment the heat of his mouth closed over the tender tip that went well beyond the pleasure she'd felt when he kissed her mouth.

She felt as if she was falling into a dark tunnel, where her entire being was focused upon that one point of intimacy, upon the heat and adhesion of his mouth, the teasing nudge of his tongue. Dizziness swirled at the edges of her consciousness. Weakness sucked at her body so that it took an effort to cling to him.

She discovered that she was panting for breath, little gasps that hovered on the edge of soft cries. The sounds seemed to drive him beyond reason. He thrust her skirts up around her waist, sliding his hand between her legs as he had before, nudging her thighs.

Near mindless with unfamiliar sensations by now, she was slow to react to that gentle instruction, but as she felt his fingers push through the slit in her pantalets, she moved her legs apart to allow him better access. The movement parted the seam where her nether lips met, opening so that the sensitive inner flesh was exposed to his exploration.

Breathing as raggedly as she was, he released her long enough to scoop her other breast free and fastened his mouth over that tip before sliding his hand downward again to explore her femininity. She gasped, arching upward as his finger traced the sensitive cleft, stroking her and finally settling on the tiny nub of flesh at the very edge, massaging it gently.

A small cry escaped her before she could think to contain it. He lifted his head from her breast at once, covering her mouth, absorbing the little cries he rung from her with each movement of his finger. The muscles low in her belly began to quake, clenching and releasing rhythmically. A sense of desperation grew inside of her as her entire body seemed to wind tighter and tighter with tension.

He slipped a knee between her parted thighs, then stiffened, a low groan that was more pain than pleasure rumbling from his chest. Abruptly, he pulled away from her and sprawled flat of his back once more, his eyes squeezed tightly shut.

Stunned by his sudden withdrawal, it took Demi several moments to recover enough to figure out what had happened. "My lord?"

He cursed beneath his breath. "My leg," he said between clenched teeth.

Dismay filled her. She glanced down at his leg, discovering in the process that he'd thrown the covers off and he was completely bare. Protruding from a thatch of dark hair low on his belly was the member she'd felt before. It looked a great deal like a stallion's member ... and a great deal different. It was certainly not as large, which was a source of relief, but far larger than she'd realized it would be. Did she have an opening on her body large enough to accommodate that, she wondered?

The thought made her femininity clench, removing any doubt from her mind of what particular part of her body yearned to be filled with his engorged flesh. Tentatively, she reached down to touch it. As her fingers tentatively explored the heated length, it jerked, grew harder and broader and longer before her eyes. A wave of heat went through her, and wonder.

He caught her exploring hand. "As much as it grieves me to tease you and leave you in need--and myself for that matter--I'm afraid my damnable leg will not allow me to pleasure either of us," he said roughly.

She glanced up at him, but even though her eyes had adjusted to the gloom, she could tell little about his features. Shadows lay across his face, but she could see the heated gleam in his eyes, and frustration. She lay her cheek over his pounding heart, then turned her head to place a kiss there. "Is there no way, my lord?"

He tipped her chin up, studying her a long moment, and pushed her skirts up. Catching one leg, he guided her until she was sitting astride him. She splayed her hands on his chest, looking down at him a little doubtfully. Reaching up, he hooked a hand behind her head and drew her down for a deep kiss. She felt his other hand moving between them, pushing the fabric of her pantalets aside. Something hard and rounded, nudged against her.

She tensed as she realized what it was, felt him stretching her as he slowly inserted it.

Her heart hammering in her chest with both fear and anticipation, she held herself perfectly still, waiting to see what he would do next. He grasped her hips, pressing her down and back in counter to the direction of his own hips. Her flesh resisted the intrusion but the pressure intensified and slowly but surely she felt him moving deeper and deeper inside of her.

He stopped finally, releasing her lips and panting raggedly.

This could not be all, she thought doubtfully, feeling as if she'd missed something very important.

He caught her face between his hands. "It will most likely hurt you when I breach your maiden head," he said harshly.

She'd heard people speak of such, but she hadn't realized there actually *was* a barrier inside of her. Fear touched her, but she nodded her understanding, bracing herself. He wrapped his arms around her, holding her tightly against him. "I should not take it."

Warmth flowed through her that had nothing to do with the tension of desire he'd created in her. "It would mean more to me to give it to you than you could possibly know," she whispered.

He kissed her, tenderly at first, and then with more fire, stoking the desire that had begun to wane. Stroking his hands along her back, he cupped her buttocks, shifting so that his engorged member slid back and forth inside of her, slowly, caressing the inner walls of her femininity. The tension of before built rapidly. Her muscles seemed to relax, cupping around his sex lovingly, but without the sense of being stretched almost beyond their limits.

He caught her hips, guiding her into the rhythm that complimented his own. As the tension of fear gave way to the tension of desire, he thrust upward suddenly, hard, ripping through the barrier and sinking so deeply inside of her that she could feel his member bumping against her womb, feel his belly grinding against her nether lips. The movement sent a wave of pain through her.

She cried out into his mouth, wrenching away from him. Ripples of fiery pain ran outward from the wound, but like the spirits that had seemed to burn her belly, the fire rapidly diminished into a throbbing heat.

A sense of euphoria washed over her with the realization that he had claimed her as no other man ever would, joined his body with her own in complete possession. Tentatively, she moved against him as he'd shown her before. Ripples of both pain and pleasure raked through her as she felt his swollen member slip along her tender passage. She concentrated on the pleasure, knowing from his ragged gasps that her movements pleased him. He caught her hips, urging her to move faster. She followed his silent instructions, focused her attention completely upon every faintest sign that a certain speed or movement increased his pleasure. She was hardly aware that her own pleasure kept pace, until she felt a burgeoning inside of her, as if something momentous was striving to break free.

As her arms tired, she pushed upward until she was sitting upright. The position drove him more deeply inside of her and she threw her head back, basking in the wealth of exquisite sensation that wrapped around and threaded through her, almost seeming to consume her, bouncing gently as she rose and fell. He grasped her hips, lifting to meet her with more and more desperation.

Abruptly, he grabbed her, pulling her down and capturing one of her nipples in his mouth, sucking hard as he hove upward, driving deep. Something shattered blindingly inside of her, an explosion of such wonderful, powerful pleasure that she gasped as it thundered through her. Inside her, she felt his manhood jerk, felt a wash of heat as his seed spilled inside of her, coating her womb and her passage.

Weak in the aftermath, she collapsed against him, struggling to catch her breath. His arms tightened around her back and across her buttocks as he held her crushingly, arching his hips to thrust deeply inside of her again and again until the spasms ceased and he lay as limply as she did.

Her sense of self was slow in returning, awareness of her surroundings giving way little by little until her senses began to focus beyond her own pounding heart, the heat and dampness of his skin beneath her cheek, his ragged breath, slowly returning to normal. Reluctance shivered over her, but she realized that she had stayed far longer than she should have, knew Sarah must be wondering what was keeping her.

"I must go, my lord," she whispered finally.

His arms tightened, as if he would refuse to release her. Finally, however, as if with great reluctance of his own, he loosened his hold. "Come to me tomorrow," he said hoarsely.

She kissed him lightly on the shoulder. "Mr. Fitzhugh is bound to wonder why I'm so anxious to gather your laundry."

He speared his fingers through her hair, dislodging her cap. "I'll make certain he takes himself off."

Chuckling, she dropped a light kiss to his shoulder and pulled away. He stopped her, catching her face between his palms and kissing her lingeringly. She was breathless by the time he released her and aware that his member, sated and limp only moments before, had come to attention once more. "I can only promise that I will try," she said, straightening her cap and moving off of him, careful not to jar his injured leg. When she'd gained the floor once more, she gathered up the laundry.

He caught her skirt, halting her when she began to move away. "I should be horsewhipped for what I just did to you. I didn't hurt you?"

She smiled, even though she doubted he could see it. "Don't say that. You're no more at fault than I am and … you gave me far more pleasure than pain, my lord."

He shook his head. "I should not have asked that of you before. Don't come. It's too risky."

Demi felt a sinking of dismay. "I…."

"You will regret this by morning … and most likely hate me."

She swallowed against a sudden lump in her throat. "Never. Come what may."

"Not even if you should find I have given you a child?"

It hadn't even occurred to her that he might, but such joy washed through her on the instant that she knew she wanted that with absolute desperation. "Most especially not then."

Disentangling her skirts from his fist, she moved across the room, opened the door and glanced down the hallway. Only one servant was in the hall now, and that one had slumped toward the floor and was sound asleep. Slipping out, she closed the door carefully behind her and rushed on tiptoe to her own room.

Sarah sat straight up in bed the moment she closed the door behind her. "I thought I would die of fright, Miss Demitria! Ye were gone so long I was certain ye'd been caught an' expectin' yer aunt to drag me from yer bed any moment!"

A blush climbed instantly into Demi's cheeks. Fortunately, the room was quite dark and she knew Sarah could not see it. She looked down at the bundle in her arms, even though she knew Sarah would not be able to see her lie in her gaze. "He woke. We talked ... and I lost track of the time. I'm sorry I worried you."

Irritably, Sarah scrambled from the bed and began to strip off Demi's night clothes. Settling the bundle of laundry, Demi followed suit, tossing Sarah's clothes to her as she removed them.

Sarah sniffed suspiciously when she dragged the gown over her head and tightened the lacing in the front. "Seems to me ye might've done a sight more than talk, considering how long ye was gone. Don't tell me ye weren't kissin' an' lovin' on him, for I can smell his after shave on me gown."

Demi glanced at Sarah self-consciously. "It was only the one," she lied.

Sarah didn't look much as if she believed her, but it was obvious she was anxious to be gone. Sniffing irritably, she moved across the room and collected the laundry. "Ye'd best get in bed before yer aunt *does* decide to come check on ye."

Nodding, Demi raced across the room and hopped into the bed, pulling the covers up. "The 'guard's' asleep."

Sarah eased the door open and peeked down the hallway. Nodding, she went out and closed the door.

Demi fell back onto her pillows, smiling up at the darkened ceiling. The blood still surged through her, making it difficult to compose herself for sleep. She knew very well that she should not feel so elated. She should feel shame. She should be worried, embarrassed, guilty. She had given herself to Garrett when she was already promised to another.

She would be damned to hell fire, condemned by everyone if it ever became known. Jonathan Flemming was going to fly into a tearing rage the moment he discovered his prize, his wife, had belonged to another before him.

She was fiercely glad of it.

She might not be able to prevent them from forcing her to marry him, but she had at least had the joy of giving herself to the man she wanted, and she had the added joy of knowing that there was some possibility that she might, even now, be carrying his child.

Chapter Ten

Far from discovering a wealth of regrets once the sun rose and spilled the unforgiving light of day into her room, Demi woke with a sense of well being that only increased when she felt the tenderness between her thighs that reminded her that Garrett had claimed her as his own.

He didn't realize it of course. He'd thought she was one of the maids, and that knowledge was the only cloud on her horizon. Resolutely, she dismissed it. She might not have known what it was like to lay with a man before last night, but she was certainly not ignorant of the ways of men. Her aunt had lamented the tendency of men to yield to their baser instincts on more than one occasion, warning both Demi and Phoebe that it was a lady's duty to hold them at bay.

Now that she'd experienced it, she understood perfectly why men had such difficulty denying the demands of their body. Anything that gave one so much pleasure would be very hard to resist indeed. Only thinking of the things he'd made her feel the night before, made her body hum to life and begin to yearn for more.

She supposed, given her new insight, she should make the effort to forgive Jonathan Flemming's trespass, but she found she was still revolted at the thought. She had not wanted him. She made it abundantly clear that it gave her no pleasure at all to have him maul her in that way, and he had completely ignored her. Not for one moment did she believe that he had 'lost his head'. He'd simply not considered her feelings on the matter of any importance.

He would not, she knew, once he had made her his wife, but that didn't bear thinking of.

Dismissing it with an effort, she climbed from the bed and moved to the washstand. It was then that she discovered the evidence of Garrett's possession of her body. She stared down at the cloth in dismay, wondering worriedly if she'd soiled Sarah's gown, as well.

Sarah would know instantly what the blood meant. Her menses were not due for another week, at least, and Sarah knew her cycle as well as she did.

Cringing at the thought of discovery, she slipped her pantalets off and washed the stains out of the fabric the best she could. She was not in the habit of doing her own laundry, however, and didn't know what to do with the pantalets when she'd finished. Turning, she studied the room for a hiding place and finally moved to the bed and stuffed the evidence beneath the mattress.

Doubt seized her almost at once. What if one of the maids dragged them out when she changed the bedding?

They wouldn't have to see the telltale stains that remained to realize she would not have tried to hide them if she wasn't guilty of something. Feeling under the mattress, she dragged the damp pantalets out again and rushed over to the armoire, wadding them into a tight little ball and piling everything in the bottom of the armoire on top of them.

The door opened just as she finished and she jerked guiltily. Straightening, she slammed the door of the armoire and glanced quickly toward her bedroom door. Sarah was studying her with a mixture of suspicion and surprise. "What're ye up to now, Miss?"

Demi blushed, but let out a gusty breath of relief. "Nothing. I just thought you were Aunt Alma."

Sarah nodded, but the suspicion didn't completely disappear from her eyes. "I've brought ye something to break yer fast. Lady Moreland's decided to be pleased with yer performance last eve. She says if ye can comport yerself like a lady, yer allowed to come downstairs again today."

Demi bit her lip at the comment, blushing harder as it instantly connected in her mind to wonder if Garrett had been pleased with her 'performance'. She rather thought he had been and the thought brought a smile to her lips.

Sarah sniffed irritably, and Demi subdued the smile, following her back across the room and climbing into the bed. Sarah settled the tray carefully across her lap. "Ye might want to consider stayin' in yer room after all."

Demi glanced at her curiously. "Why?"

Sarah rolled her eyes. "It's as plain as the nose on yer face that ye were up to a bit more than cuddlin' an' kissin' last night. I've never seen a maid who looked more thoroughly bedded, or more pleased about it."

Demi looked at her self-consciously, trying to think of something to say.

Sarah held her hand up. "Ye needn't waste yer breath. Ye'll not convince me, nor nobody else if yer gonna be goin' around with that sappy look on yer face."

Demi chuckled uneasily. "I'm not going to fall for it, so you may as well stop fishing."

"I ain't fishin'. I'm just sayin' you needn't go to a lot of trouble thinkin' up a good tale on my account. I won't believe it, an' I'm not the one ye have to convince anyways."

Demi ate thoughtfully after Sarah had left, wondering if Sarah really could tell, or if she was just trying to trip her up. She finally decided, maybe, that Sarah *could* tell. She felt different. She supposed it was because she was truly happy for the first time in longer than she could remember.

Her aunt might not be suspicious if she seemed resigned, but she would certainly think Demi was up to something if she seemed happy.

She would also be suspicious, however, if Demi remained in her room, or think that Demi was still sulking, in which case she might devise another punishment. Demi finally decided it would be best to go downstairs, regardless of what Sarah had said. She needn't spend a great deal of time in her aunt's company, or her cousins' for that matter. Phoebe and Geoffrey both had their own friends and their own interests.

She discovered when she went downstairs that she was wrong on all counts. Her aunt had planned a small party for the 'young people', an excursion to the lake for a picnic--the same lake Jonathan Flemming had taken her to. Demi was immediately sorry she'd decided to go downstairs at all. She could have flat refused to go, of course, but she knew what the end result of that would be--three more days of being locked in her room, with no chance of seeing Lord Wyndham, whom she learned would be leaving at the end of the week.

Dejection instantly washed away the last of the glow that had lingered from their night together. With the ordeal of the 'promised treat' on top of that announcement, Demi had no trouble at all behaving as if she was subdued. She was.

It was a testament to just how much she adored Garrett that she did not immediately return to her room. Phoebe and her aunt were going. Jonathan and Esmeralda, and Mr. Collins and his sister, Miss Elizabeth Collins, would also be joining the expedition, but Demi didn't trust either her aunt or Jonathan Flemming. Despite her aunt's assertion that the primary goal of the picnic was to dampen the possible gossip stemming from Demi's hastily put together marriage, she had the uneasy feeling that she would be thrust into yet another compromising situation with Flemming.

There was no need for such a thing, of course. She had been so thoroughly compromised now it would be difficult to further damage her reputation, and they must be as aware as she was that the well witnessed aftermath of the incident had thoroughly trapped her.

Regardless, she knew Flemming had been determined to get her alone again and since she believed her aunt had had a hand in the first incident--or at the very least had simply turned a blind eye--she didn't trust her aunt to thwart his intentions.

Knowing her options were limited, she put up no demure, but she resolved to refuse any attempt by Flemming to get her off to himself.

They hit their first hurtle when they began to load up in the carriages. They'd arranged to take three carriages. When Demi tried to join her aunt and cousin Phoebe, her aunt immediately objected. "Don't be absurd. You will ride with your fiancé. Esmeralda can ride with us."

Demi's eyes narrowed. "If I am to ride with Mr. Flemming, then Esmeralda can ride with us."

Alma Moreland studied her for a moment. "You are a

tiresome girl. I shall enjoy the peace when you are no longer my responsibility."

Demi had to bite her tongue to keep from informing her aunt that she lived for the day, but as badly as she wanted to tell her aunt how she felt about it, she had resolved not to give her aunt any further justification for keeping her a prisoner in her own room. Turning away from her aunt's carriage, she looped her arm through Esme's and headed for Jonathan's carriage.

The smile he gave her when she stopped beside the carriage made her long to whack him a few times about the head with her parasol. She'd brought her parasol explicitly for that purpose, should the need arise. Setting her jaw, she allowed him to help her into the carriage.

"I thought Lady Moreland had invited you to join her and Phoebe," he said as he turned to his daughter.

Esme glanced at Demi and then her father. "But, I don't like Lady Moreland, papa. I thought I'd ride with you and Demitria. She *is* to be my new step mama, after all."

Demi, who'd been staring at the horse's ears in fuming silence, turned and looked at her friend in stunned surprise. Flemming obviously didn't particularly care for Esme's humor. He was as red as a radish. Gritting his teeth, he helped Esme into the back seat of the carriage without another word, then stalked around the carriage and climbed in.

Demi bit her lip to contain a smile as she twisted around to look at Esme. Esme winked at her, grinned and settled back with the air of one who was already enjoying herself tremendously.

When they arrived at the lake, they discovered that the servants had arrived before them and were in the process of setting up the picnic. Phoebe suggested they take a stroll around the lake and immediately attached herself to Mr. Collins. Flemming offered his arm. Ignoring it, Demi looped her arm through Esme's and asked her if she'd read any good novels lately. Miss Elizabeth Collins joined Demi and Esme, and Flemming was left to lend his support to Lady Moreland.

Books were more dear to Esme's heart than anything

else in life, and she talked at length about those she'd read most recently, relieving Demi and Elizabeth of the need to do anything more than listen. Ordinarily, Demi would have been nearly as enthusiastic, but she couldn't help but wonder what Esme thought about her father's marriage plans. She had not spoken of it before today … and, until she had, Demi had not even considered that her marriage to Jonathan would make her Esme's step mother.

She knew Esme missed her mother fiercely and wondered if it distressed her to think of Demi becoming mistress of the home that had been her mother's. She could scarcely approach so delicate a subject with Elizabeth Collins present, but she worried that the marriage might create a rift between them.

Growing bored with the discussion of books, Elizabeth detached herself after a little while and joined her brother and Phoebe. Flemming took the opportunity to draw even with Esme and Demi.

Demi sent him a deadly look. "We can not walk four abreast. The path is too narrow."

"Then walk with me."

"Esme and I are discussing books."

His eyes narrowed. "As fascinating a subject as that is, you and I have things to discuss, as well."

"Oh? I was certain you and Aunt Alma had already made all the arrangements that needed to be made."

"Traditionally, the bride and groom plan their wedding trip together," he said with determined patience.

Demi lifted her brows. "Forced marriages are traditional?"

Esme divided a frightened look between her father and Demi. "I believe I will head back now."

"A very good idea," Demi said, turning with her and pushing past her aunt, who'd been forced to drop back due to the narrowness of the path they'd been following. To her relief, Jonathan made no attempt to stop her. Instead, he offered his arm to Alma Moreland once more and the four of them returned to the picnic site.

Except for the deadly looks her aunt sent her way and Jonathan's coldly assessing looks throughout the meal, the remainder of the picnic went off fairly well. Demi looked forward to the return trip to the Abbey with more than a little dread, however, certain that she would once again have to fend off Flemming's attempts to get her alone. To her surprise and relief, he didn't.

The bad moment came when they arrived home once more. Everyone had loaded up in the same carriages they'd arrived in, but Flemming managed to see to it that theirs was the last in the procession. Since the carriages ahead of them were kicking up a good deal of dust, he dropped back. The end result was that everyone had already entered the Abbey by the time they arrived.

Demi knew Flemming had been roiling ever since the walk along the lake, although he'd made every attempt to appear completely oblivious to her determined snubs. He pulled the carriage to a halt on the drive before the Abbey, set the hand brake, looped the reins around it, then got down and walked around to help Demi alight. When Esme would have followed them, he fixed her with a look. "You will wait in the carriage. We will not be staying."

Grasping Demi's arm, he walked her beyond earshot of Esme and pulled her to a halt. "I have tolerated a good deal from you, Demitria, but know this, I will expect complete compliance from you once we are wed."

Demi gave him a level look, despite the fact that she was quaking in her shoes. "You will have nothing less … and nothing more," she said tightly.

"You do not want to engage in a battle of wills with me. I can assure you, you'll lose."

Demi stared at him a long moment. "I already lost or there would *be* no wedding, but don't congratulate yourself over it. Aunt Alma won the first round, not you," she said, snatching her arm from his grip and stalking into the manor.

She had to stop to compose herself once she was safely inside. Fully expecting to find that her aunt was laying in wait for her to give her a thorough dressing down, she was vastly relieved to discover that she'd retired to her room to rest. Very likely it was only a short reprieve, however, and she decided to retire to her own room to rest before she had to rejoin the battle with her aunt.

In her room, she discarded her gown and lay down in her shift, but she discovered that rest was not an option. Jonathan Flemming had frightened her far more than she was willing to let on, far more than he had when he'd attempted to inflict his ardor on her. She reminded herself that she had known all along that he was just as determined to control her every move and thought as her Aunt Alma was, and would be far more dangerous, if for no other reason than that he would be her husband. She realized, though, that she had not fully accepted it before. Somehow, she supposed in the back of her mind, she'd been certain that she was exaggerating the situation because of her distaste for him, that he couldn't possibly be as bad as she'd imagined. The conversation at the door had left her in no doubt that he was. She'd gotten the distinct impression that he was looking forward to breaking her to his will.

She supposed she would have been far better off if she had behaved meekly from the start and at least given the impression that she would be easy to control. She didn't think that that would've made him not want her, because she was fairly certain that she'd also been correct about him wanting her because her family connections would raise his status in the community.

The fact that she'd shown herself to be headstrong and willful had appealed to him on another level, however. Before, it was possible that he had had no particular interest in her beyond the connection, but she had challenged him. He would make her life a living nightmare until he was satisfied that he had asserted his dominance and completely broken her spirit.

She wished desperately that she could go to Garrett for comfort, but there was no chance at all of that before everyone had retired for the night, probably very little even then. She thought it very unlikely that Sarah would help her again as she had the night before, not when she suspected what had happened between her and Garrett.

If she had not been so fearful of being left alone with Jonathan Flemming and yet another confrontation with her aunt, the vigil in watching her might have been relaxed enough that she could slip out of her room. Unfortunately, she had, and she would be lucky if it didn't transpire that she was right back where she'd started--forbidden to leave her room at all, placed on bread and water, with Sarah barred altogether from her room.

That thought reminded her of the yardman that had been sent to nail her window shut. He hadn't. He'd risked his job by passing food to her ... and he'd left the ladder under her window. Slipping from the bed, she moved to the window and pulled the curtains back. The ladder was still beneath her window.

She was surprised her aunt hadn't noticed and had it removed, but then her aunt rarely went outside.

She began pacing the room, trying to decide if there was any way she might make use of the ladder. After developing one scenario after another, however, she was obliged to dismiss it. The ladder was too heavy, she was certain, for her to move it, no matter how determined she might be. She could use it to escape her room, but she would have to enter the manor once more in order to get to Garrett.

Unless she could convince Sarah to help her again, she would not be able to be with him. He thought she was a maid. He would not take her into his bed if he knew.

It occurred to her after a little bit that she might be able to borrow a maid's clothing from the laundry. It would most certainly be noticed if the clothing was gone for very long, but Garrett was to be leaving soon. If she could figure out a way to get the clothing to begin with, she could figure out how to get it back.

Even such a disguise wouldn't help her escape her room, however, if her aunt decided to post servants in the upper hall as she had before. One might succumb to weariness and sleep as the one the night before had. If there were two or more, most likely they would be too afraid of being reported and having to face her aunt's wrath to give in to the desire to sleep.

She decided she could only tackle one obstacle at the time. If she saw the opportunity to steal a disguise from the laundry, she would seize it and worry about the other things later.

She was surprised, but hopeful, when Sarah came in to help her dress for dinner. At least her aunt hadn't tightened down on her as of yet.

Chapter Eleven

Demi stopped abruptly in stunned surprise when she reached the parlor. Lord Wyndham, looking pale from his ordeal, and no doubt the effort of negotiating the stairs, was seated in a chair facing the door, a cane propped against the chair beside his injured leg. His eyes gleamed with warmth when he spied her, a faint smile hovering about his lips.

She smiled tentatively in return. "My lord! It's wonderful to see you up and moving about."

"Phoebe and I were just expressing our delight in seeing him so robust again!" Alma Moreland said at once, although it was obvious that she and her daughter had only just arrived in the parlor themselves.

Phoebe sent her mother a startled glance, blushed faintly at the sardonic glance Garrett sent in their direction and added, "We were certainly *thinking* that very thing. That is ... mother and I were expressing how delighted we would be to see you looking stout and hardy again on the way downstairs."

"Then I am glad that I spent the past several days hobbling about in my room so that I could impress you. I can see I wouldn't have made nearly as favorable an impression if I'd allowed the footmen to carry me down. My apologies for not rising, but I had the devil of a time getting downstairs."

Lady Moreland waved that away. "We will certainly excuse so understandable a lapse. We know very well that you're not as recovered as you would have us think. I suppose this means you are, in truth, to be leaving us soon?" Alma Moreland added but apparently decided the comment sounded far too hopeful. "We shall miss your excellent company! I would that we could prevail upon you to stay a little longer."

"Alas, I've a great deal of business that needs attending," he responded coolly. "And, in any case, I have trespassed upon your hospitality far too long as it is."

Lady Moreland smiled. "As to that, there was certainly no trespass. We have been delighted to have you. You're certain we can't persuade you? I know of at least one here at Moreland Abbey who will be very sad indeed to see you go," she said archly, leaning over to pat Phoebe's hand.

His gaze flickered from Lady Moreland to Phoebe and finally settled on Demi. Swallowing with an effort, she moved to a chair and sat, staring at her hands while she focused on subduing the knot of misery in her chest. It wasn't as if she hadn't known that he would be going after all. Despite that, however, she couldn't deny that it was an unpleasant jolt to see the actuality of preparations. She supposed it wouldn't have been so had not some dark corner of her mind held on to hope that the unhappy fate that seemed to be rushing upon her would somehow be diverted, perhaps in the eleventh hour, and she would discover that happiness was to be hers after all.

It might have been easier bear if she could simply have quelled the tiny spark of hope that refused to be extinguished, but she supposed it sprang from the happiness she'd felt in seeing and being with him. It was like a hunger. When fed, it sprang to life more readily. Whereas starvation dampened it to the point where one rarely even expected to have it appeased.

She had her memories, though. She could nurture them and keep them alive and they would bring her a taste of happiness whenever she brought them out. If she had not been so fearful of pain before, she would have had the memories of her parents to cherish. Instead, she had thrown up a wall that had sealed both the good and the bad away from her forever.

Geoffrey was the last to arrive. He took one look at Lord Wyndham and looked as if he wanted to whirl and flee upstairs again. Unfortunately, unlike Lord Wyndham, he had not arrived under his own steam. He had been carried down by the footmen, and she supposed the indignity of ordering them about to carry him upstairs once more outweighed his reluctance to endure a confrontation with Lord Wyndham.

In point of fact, tension was rife in the room, but Lord Wyndham soon set them at ease by conversing with Geoffrey as his host, rather than the man who'd shot and nearly killed him. Dinner was almost convivial. Demi strongly suspected that there was as much hysterical relief in Geoffrey, Phoebe, and Lady Morcland's banter as there was good cheer, but the liveliness lifted even her flagging spirits.

It also silenced, or at least quieted, the voices of reason in her head. She'd managed to slip into the laundry and borrow one of the upstairs maid's work dresses and cap, but she'd been assailed by guilt as much as fear as she'd scurried back upstairs to hide it. What she was doing, and intended to do, was wrong, if possible even more wrong than before. She had not intended that anything happen between them when she had slipped into Garrett's room, and even though she'd given in without a whimper of protest, she might have been able to salve her conscience with a lack of intent.

Borrowing the maid's dress to go back, knowing what would happen, in fact hoping that it would, was as premeditated as one could get.

Two wrongs did not equal one right and never would. In point of fact, as her legal guardian, her aunt had every right to settle her as she saw fit. Most guardians would have given at least some consideration to their ward's wishes, but certainly not all, and even those who did considered their age and experience were more likely to produce a compatible match than the unstable and inexperienced young could manage, given the right to choose.

She was as bound by her guardian's decision as if she'd chosen it herself, and she was willfully dishonoring it.

She'd told herself she didn't care and it didn't matter, but she knew very well that she wouldn't have had to if it didn't. She realized though, as the evening progressed, that she was willing to accept the consequences later of her actions now.

She silenced the clamoring of guilt and shame. She couldn't altogether silence the voice of fear. Her conversation with Jonathan Flemming returned again and again, and each time his words returned to her mind they frightened her more powerfully.

Garrett had known that she hadn't been with a man. Flemming would know that she had. What he might do when he learned of it didn't bear thinking of. He would almost certainly figure out that it had been Garrett she'd lain with.

Would he publicly denounce her? Call Garrett out? Beat her?

It was a terrifying thought, but unfortunately, not something that she could change now. Whether she went to Garrett one more time before he left or not, that couldn't be changed.

As fearful as she was of the possible repercussions, she couldn't be sorry for it, and when she realized that she did not wish it undone, she pushed the fear to the back of her mind determined not to allow it to torture her. She would face the consequences when she had to. She wouldn't allow her dread in the meantime to govern her actions or prevent her from making the most of the time she had left to her.

When she retired for the evening, she went about preparing for bed as usual. Sarah studied her suspiciously, but she was far too wrapped up in trying to behave 'normal' to really notice. In any case, she was certain that not asking Sarah to help her would be enough to allay Sarah's suspicions about her plans.

If she hadn't been so swamped with guilt and so nervous, she would have realized that that was exactly what *did* arouse Sarah's suspicions. Is she'd asked, and then argued and allowed Sarah to talk her out of it, Sarah would have left her with the feeling that she'd 'talked some sense into the girl'. As it was, Sarah left her feeling nearly as uneasy as Demi did.

She was too nervous to sleep. In any case, she was fearful that if she tried to doze for a little while that she wouldn't wake until morning and she would discover she'd missed her chance.

She had no clock in her room to tell her the time, and no certainty, in any case, of what time she should make the attempt. She worried over it for some time and finally recalled that it had been very dark in Garrett's room when she'd gone the night before. The single lamp, turned low, had barely spilled across the room and virtually no light had filtered in from outside. Since Garrett's room was on the same side of the house as hers, that could only have meant that the moon had at least reached its zenith by the time she'd arrived in his room.

Climbing from the bed, she went to the window to check the moon's progress. Clouds scudded across the sky, but she could see the moonlit filtering through high above the horizon. She studied it for several moments, wondering how long it would take to reach the midpoint and finally moved away from the window to the door to listen.

Lord Wyndham had still been downstairs with Lord Moreland when she and the others had come upstairs and she wondered if she shouldn't give up the idea altogether. Perhaps he'd forgotten he'd asked her to come back? Or maybe he'd changed his mind?

Despite her fears/hope to the contrary, she'd seen nothing in his eyes to make her think he realized that it had been her the night before in his room. Perhaps a sense of guilt had prompted him to rethink the matter? Few gentlemen worried about dishonoring lowly maids, but she knew that Garrett was not like that. Perhaps he'd been overcome with his needs the night before, but then worried that he might get the girl dismissed or pregnant if he pursued it?

She'd been pacing the distance between the door and the window for hours it seemed before she heard the telltale rap of his cane on the floor that told her he'd come upstairs at last. She listened until he'd gone into his room and closed the door, then moved back to the window.

The moon, she saw, was beyond her vision.

He'd stayed downstairs long past the time when she should have gone ... to warn her away, she knew. He'd told her not to risk it, but she knew what the risks were. If she was willing to chance it, surely he wouldn't send her away?

He was leaving tomorrow. Even if they allowed her to go down to see him off, she would not have a moment alone with him.

Shaking her doubts, she moved to the door once more and waited until she heard it open again and Fitzhugh's tread as he retired for the evening.

Moving to the armoire, she unearthed the maid's clothing, pulled her night gown off and struggled into the gown without bothering to don a chemise. When she'd stuffed her hair under the mob cap, she went to the door and eased it open, peering down the hallway.

She saw no sign of the footman who'd stood in the hallway since her confrontation with her aunt. Pulling the door open a little further, she leaned out to take a better look.

Either her aunt hadn't told him to watch this night, or more likely, he'd decided to take a break and had left his post.

She'd worry about that when the time came, she decided. Slipping out the door, she closed it carefully, and run on tiptoe down the hallway to Garrett's room, tapping lightly on the panel. The door was snatched open almost at once. He was wearing nothing but his breeches and she wondered if she'd interrupted him as he undressed for bed.

Leaning around her, he glanced quickly up and down the hallway. "You should go," he said in a harsh whisper, "before you're seen here."

Demi's heart dropped. "I just wanted to tell you good-bye."

He shook his head. "Last night I was drunk. It seemed perfectly reasonable to take what I wanted when you didn't protest. I'm not nearly drunk enough tonight to take that kind of chance."

Humiliation flooded her cheeks with pounding color. Nodding, she turned away. Before she could take more than a step back, however, she heard a slight sound from the direction of the stairs. Even as she whirled to look, it connected instantly in her mind that it must be the footman … and from the proximity of the sound he must already have reached the upstairs landing. She would never make it to her room before he saw her.

Apparently, Garrett realized that as well. Grasping her arm, he hauled her inside his room and closed the door.

They waited, listening tensely as he took up the position he'd assumed for the past several nights in the hallway near the head of the stairs.

Demi didn't know whether she was more frightened or more embarrassed. Garrett didn't even want her and now she was trapped in his room and unable to flee her shame. She glanced around the room. As it had been the night before, only one lamp was lit. The one beside the bed had been extinguished.

After a moment, she moved quietly away from the door. Things had gone badly enough as it was. She didn't want Garrett to see her well enough to realize that she wasn't one of the maids. As humiliated as she was, it was some comfort that at least he didn't know it was her.

Moving to the window, she pulled the curtain back and stared down at the darkened lawn. The moon had moved far enough across the sky that the area directly below was in darkness, but a little further, it lit up the lawn almost like day.

Or, perhaps, it was only the sharp contrast?

She didn't realize that Garrett had followed her until he placed his hands lightly on her shoulders. "You are trapped now, until he falls asleep--*if* he falls asleep. If not, we shall have to think of something else."

Demi stiffened at his touch. "It would be better, I think, my lord, if I gathered the laundry ... or took a tray if there is one ... and took my chances now. If he says anything, I could always say I'd been asked to bring something. If I stay longer, I'll not have even so flimsy an excuse as that."

"I have the gravest of doubts that your disguise will fool him even for a second. It did not fool me, and I was dead drunk. Of course, I would know you if I were blind, and we can hope that his little excursion downstairs was to have a little nip.... In which case, he is bound to go back for another before long."

A deluge of conflicting thoughts and emotions went through her at his words. Foremost among them was a sense of deep hurt. It was almost better to think that he hadn't known who she was than to think that he had and the only reason he'd made love to her was because he was too drunk to consider the consequences. "You did not seem drunk," she said cautiously.

He snorted. "Because I was in bed, instead of staggering around on my bum leg? Trust me. I was three sheets to the wind."

Demi cleared her throat. "But ... you didn't even slur your words."

"Unfortunately, your timing was all too perfect. A little earlier, and I'd have had the sense to send you away. A little later, and I'd have been too far gone to be a threat to you."

Demi bowed her head, fighting the urge to weep. She wished fervently that she had not come now. His refusal to let her in was humiliating enough, but to find that what had happened between them the night before was merely the result of too much drink, too much carnal need, and not enough judgment was far worse. Despite everything, she'd been overjoyed by the knowledge that Garrett had been her first and that no one could take that away from her, whatever else she was powerless to prevent. She drew in a deep, shuddering breath. "I'm sorry. It was unconscionable of me to put you in such an uncomfortable position, especially when you've been so kind to me.

"I didn't mean for that to happen. Truly. I just wanted to be certain that you were all right. You'd been so ill. I was afraid that Sarah had only told me you were getting better to keep me from worrying.

"As for tonight ... well, I only came to tell you good-bye, in case I didn't see you before you left tomorrow. And ... well, because I didn't want to have to behave as a polite stranger because of Aunt Alma."

He removed his hands from her shoulders, moving slightly away from her. "The regrets have set in I see."

She flicked a glance at him, but she didn't actually make eye contact. Instead, she looked away again, put a little more distance between them as she moved toward the chair.

The unfortunate truth was that she didn't regret it, but he, obviously, did. It hurt that he did, and because it hurt, it also made her angry. Despite the urge to tell him the unvarnished truth, the temptation to wound him in return was stronger still. She shrugged, moving away from the chair. She would have to look at him if she sat down, and she didn't think she could look him in the eye and lie to him.

"I expect Jonathan will make me regret it, but it is a fitting revenge, all things considered. Don't you think?"

"You made love to me to spite Jonathan Flemming?"

Faintly, the smell of strong spirits wafted warningly past her nostrils. He'd been downstairs for hours, no doubt with Geoffrey, imbibing freely. She knew from seeing Geoffrey in his cups that men were prone to dangerous and very unpredictable mood swings when they imbibed. She should have been warned by the tone of his voice, but she was too hurt and angry to pay any mind. "He is my aunt's choice, not mine. I may be powerless to stop them, but I will at least have the satisfaction that he will realize on our wedding night that someone has been before him. And then there is the strong possibility that I might even now be with child. He will hate me as I hate him each time he has to look at another man's child." Always assuming he didn't kill her for her perfidy and disguise it to look like an accident ... or beat her until she lost the child and all chance of ever conceiving again.

At that moment, she almost relished the thought that Garrett would have to live with her death on his conscience ... assuming he had one or even suspected Flemming had killed her because of him.

"I have misjudged you. You are a cunning little jade," he growled in a harsh whisper.

The comment sent another shaft of pain and anger through her. Demi flushed. She turned to face him but found she still couldn't meet his gaze. "You are angry because you think I used you, when you were only using me to slake your lust?" she gasped, outraged. "How very *male* of you! But as it happens, your opinion of me is of no consequence. I'm just surprised you didn't call me a slut, but I expect that's next. I suppose I am, for I thoroughly enjoyed it. You are very good, even drunk. I must suppose it comes from a great deal of practice."

He caught her in two strides, jerking her up against his

body. "That's enough, Demi."

She struggled to pull away. Realizing almost immediately that she couldn't free herself unless he was willing to release her, she glared at his bare chest. "I suppose I should apologize for my clumsiness. I've had no practice myself, but that can certainly be remedied. Married women, I understand, have far more freedom for this sort of thing. How long should I wait, do you think, before I can take a lover?"

Gripping her shoulders, he set her far enough away from him that he could look down at her. Demi refused to lift her head to meet his gaze, however. "Have it your way, then. I'll give you what you came for," he growled. Gripping her chin almost painfully, he tilted her face up, lowered his head and covered her mouth angrily, silencing her at last in a kiss that was meant to be punishing and hurtful.

Chapter Twelve

As angry and hurt as she was, Demi welcomed his punishing kiss with fierce gladness. She wanted to drive him over the edge into madness, wanted to push him until he hurt her so that she could hate him. Instead, desire rushed through her the moment she felt his hard mouth, felt the ravishment of his tongue as it skated over hers possessively, tangled with her own, began a wild, primal mating dance as he sought to dominate her. For many moments, she could not think at all, couldn't catch her breath with the influx of heat and desire, like heady wine, racing through her blood. Driven by both need and anger, she clenched her hands, digging her nails into his chest, kneading his flesh like a contented cat. He shifted away from the pain, kissing her more savagely still. The moment he did, she slipped one hand downward and cupped his sex.

He stiffened, but as she rubbed the palm of her hand over the distended ridge, imitating the movements of their lovemaking the night before, he placed one hand over hers, pressing her palm hard against his length. A shudder went through him, a quaking, as one who holds himself so tensely they strain near the breaking point. His breathing grew ragged, labored. Abruptly, he tore his mouth from hers, struggled with the tie at the neck of the gown briefly, then caught the neck of her dress with both hands and snapped the tie, baring her almost to the waist as the torn lacing slipped from its grommets. Her unfettered breasts fell free with a gentle bounce, her nipples growing tight instantly, pouting with need.

He caught a breast in each hand, leaning down and suckling first one and then the other, kneading them. Demi sucked in her breath at the first contact of his heated mouth, feeling a wave of dizziness wash over her. Tangling her fingers in his dark hair, she cupped his head, urging him to lavish the teasing torment of his mouth and tongue on her nipples, scarcely aware of the whimper of protest that edged its way up her throat when he abandoned one for the other.

Catching her waist, he lifted her, swinging her around and laying her back on the edge of the bed. She dug her fingers into the bedding, gripping it tightly as her head swum. He followed her down, leaning over her, an arm braced on the bed on either side of her as he kissed her mouth briefly, then moved along her throat to capture one trembling peak of her breast in his mouth once more. If possible, the sensations were even more intense. She found that she was gasping so hard it was more like hoarse cries than gasps scoring her throat.

After a few moments, she realized she lay half on and half off the bed. Gripping the sheets, she pulled herself backwards until she felt the mattress beneath her hips as he moved his mouth from her breasts to her neck once more. He caught her hips, trapping her on the edge of the bed, and she opened her eyes to look up at him in confusion. Grasping her skirts, he dragged them up, bunching them about her waist.

He lifted his head then, catching her gaze as he slipped a hand beneath the waist of her pantalets and very deliberately snapped the tie. She gasped, torn between a fervor that matched the taut desire in his face, and dismay at the anger that she saw still seethed beneath the surface. Her uneasiness increased as he pulled the pantalets from her and tossed them aside, then reached for the opening of his breeches, unsheathing his erect member.

Catching her legs with his hands, he hooked her heels on the edge of the bed and leaned over her. She felt the rounded head of his member nudging along her sensitive cleft and tensed with expectation, feeling a renewed burst of hunger for him that chased her doubts into abeyance. She wanted him. She didn't care at this moment about anything beyond feeling him deeply inside of her, a part of herself and yet excitingly unfamiliar, as well, his hardness engulfed by her yielding flesh, the heat and strength of his body possessing even as it caressed, taking from her even as it gave.

She reached for him as she felt her flesh yield to his pressure, felt him sliding slowly into her damp passage, but she found that the position prevented her from touching him. It was enthralling and at the same time disconcerting to feel him joining his body with hers and yet so distant that only those two points converged. Panting, dizzy with the pounding of her heart and the rush of blood through her, she gripped the covers as he leaned forward, slowly moving deeper and deeper inside of her, stretching her resistant muscles, until he'd claimed her depths. He withdrew almost as slowly, until no more than the rounded head of his member remained imbedded inside her, then thrust again, more smoothly and easily as her body adjusted to him.

She squeezed her eyes closed, allowing her mind to focus on the stroke of his hard member along her passage as he began to thrust and retreat more quickly. A glorious tension began to build inside of her, vibrating along her nerve endings delightfully. Mindlessly, she reached for him again, the need to feel the closeness of his body almost as intense as her urge to struggle toward release. She touched his fingers where they gripped her legs, touched his hands, but he was too caught up in his own battle toward release to respond to her silent plea.

As if her touch had driven his own hunger beyond his control, he began thrusting harder and harder, pounding into her so hard she began to slip away from him, felt her body driven slowly, inch by inch, along the mattress. She dug her heels in, gripping the bed covering tightly in her fists as he released her legs and caught her around the waist.

Abruptly, he leaned over her. Slipping an arm beneath her, he moved her further into the bed, following her. Bracing his arms on either side of her, he pushed inside of her once more. She gasped as she felt her body rise swiftly and hover on the brink of fulfillment as he thrust into her again, immediately setting the hard, pounding rhythm of before. She hovered so long on the edge, fearful that she would fall over, and fearful that she would not, that when the pleasure suddenly thrust her over the brink into an explosion of blinding pleasure, she cried out, half in surprise, and half in shock at the intensity of it.

As if he had been holding himself back, awaiting that moment, he uttered a guttural growl and stiffened, slamming into her in several shuddering thrusts and finally pushing deep and holding himself perfectly still as he gasped to catch his breath.

Coolness washed over Demi as her body floated back to earth. She shivered, realizing suddenly that he had held himself away from her even after he'd pushed her up onto the bed, that he still held himself away from her.

The sense of euphoria began to thin like mist before the wind, a cold wind that brought disenchantment and reality crashing in on her.

Weak in the aftermath of his own release, he withdrew from her and dropped onto the bed beside her. Almost simultaneously, the door opened. Both of them stiffened, whirling toward the sound instinctively. Fortunately, Garrett was far quicker to realize the threat than she was. He blocked her view of the door, thereby blocking the view of the person who'd entered the room.

"My lord! I beg you pardon. I heard a noise and thought you might need assistance."

"Out!" Garrett roared furiously.

The servant backed out, slamming the door behind him. Frozen in shocked horror, Demi listened as his footsteps disappeared in the direction of her aunt's room.

"We are in the soup now, and make no mistake," Garrett muttered. "Or I am, at least."

Demi glanced at him sharply in confusion.

His look was sardonic. "I could not have compromised you more if I had planned it that way. Or, perhaps someone did?"

Despite the lingering aftereffects of their lovemaking, and the fear of being caught, Demi had no trouble instantly connecting his meaning. Her lips tightened. Without a word, she sat up and began to hastily adjust her clothing. He'd broken the tie at the bodice. It was too short now to put it to rights. She contented herself with lacing it to the tops of her breasts and tying a short bow. The pantalets, she discovered when she climbed off the bed and stepped into them, were in pretty much the same condition. Bunching the cloth, the tied the open edges together in the place of the broken lacing.

After studying her a long moment, Garrett had gotten off the bed and moved to the door, belatedly shoving the bolt home. She glanced at him.

He shrugged. "It will give us a few moments ... maybe."

For what, she wondered? Dread? Regrets?

There was no way out of the room beyond the door Garrett had just bolted. She could unlock it and race to her room, but that wasn't likely to help at all. Even now, she could hear the servant tapping at her aunt's door to report--he might not know it had been her, but he certainly knew someone from the house was in Garrett's bed. One way or another, they would soon know who.

Turning, she paced to the window and pulled the drapes aside. It was dark beneath the window, but she didn't need the light to know there was no way she could safely reach the ground. If she could, she had a chance at least. Assuming her aunt didn't race to her room immediately and check on her, she could climb the ladder the yardman had left, but she rather thought it more likely that her aunt would go directly to her room than come to Garrett's. She would not want to confront him on such a thing without having some sort of proof of who was with him.

"Thinking of jumping?"

Demi sent him a look but decided to ignore than comment as she had his earlier suggestion that she'd planned this to force his hand. She supposed she had no one to blame but herself. If she hadn't been so hurt and angry as to make those remarks before about Flemming, he might not have been so quick to assume the worst of her, to believe that she was just devious and manipulative enough to have decided to seduce him so that he'd be forced to do the gentlemanly thing and marry her. It still rankled. Unreasonable as she knew it was, she resented that he'd been so easily convinced that she was inherently evil.

Of course, if his judgment had not already been impaired by the fact that he was pretty well into his cups, she probably wouldn't have seduced him so easily either.

She was still angry, upset that he was only human after all, that he wasn't as astute, or as perfect, as she'd believed, and irritated with herself for trying to find excuses for him, even now, when he was being a complete horse's ass.

"You are not, surely, that loathe to have me instead of Flemming?"

He was seated on the bed, propped up by a mound of pillows, his legs crossed before him. She sent him a narrow-eyed glare and succumbed to the urge to lower herself to his level. "Truthfully, at the moment I don't see a ha'penny's worth of difference between the two of you," she snapped angrily and marched from the window to the door, putting her ear to it. There was a great deal of activity down the hall now and above too in the servants' quarters in the attic. Her aunt had sent the serving man to check the maids.

She was tempted to ease the door open to see if the hall had cleared and there might be a chance of dashing, unnoticed, to her room. Unnerved by the notion, she hesitated, gnawing her lower lip while she considered if the timing was the best she could hope for. A sound from the other side of the room captured her attention, and she glanced toward Garrett. She saw that he was looking at the window.

Her heart skipped a beat, but a surge of hope rushed through her. Sarah would almost certainly have put together the commotion. Leaving the door, she moved to the window again, this time pushing it up and leaning out. In the shadows below, she could see movement. "Who's there?" she whispered as loudly as she dared.

"Shhh! Fitzhugh's movin' the ladder."

In a few moments, Sarah's worried face appeared through the shadows. "I hadn't figured to need this bleedin' thing, but I'm that glad I told Jamie to leave it." She climbed over the window sill and into the room. "Down with ye now, Miss, while there's still time."

Demi stared at Sarah. "What are you going to do?"

"Lady Dragon's expectin' to find a female in here. I wouldn't want ta disappoint her."

Demi grabbed Sarah's arm. "Don't! She'll dismiss you without a reference. I know you mean well, but I can't let you take the blame for me."

Sarah shook her head. "Go on, now. I'll be fine. Don't ye be worryin' about me. Mr. Fitzhugh has promised to find a place for me, an' I know he's a man of his word. Not that I wouldn't have done it anyway, mind you. I'm careful with my money and I've a bit tucked away for emergencies."

Still, Demi hesitated. "I'll miss you, Sarah. Maybe ... maybe I could convince Mr. Flemming to hire you on," she said doubtfully.

Sarah patted her cheek. "We'll worry about that later, if ye don't mind. I climbed into yer room and barricaded the door, but it won't take them long to break it down if they're a mind to. Go before we both get tossed out on our ear. Ye can't do me any good if ye've no place ta lay yer own head."

Nodding, Demi threw a last look at Garrett. He was sitting on the edge of the bed now, she saw, frowning at her and Sarah. Without a word, she turned her attention to her task, climbed carefully through the window, and made her way down the ladder shakily. When she'd stepped off, Fitzhugh caught the ladder and moved it down to her window.

It wasn't nearly as nerve wracking, she discovered, to climb up the ladder as it had been to go down it. When she'd climbed through, Fitzhugh took the ladder down and disappeared into the darkness with it. Letting out a tremulous sigh of relief, Demi tugged the gown off, hid it in the bottom of her armoire and dragged her night gown over her head.

Staring at her bed uncertainly for several moments, she finally tiptoed across the room and listened at the door. A few moments later, she heard footsteps coming quickly down the servants' stairs, striding down the hall and a few moments later a low voiced conversation between the servant and her aunt. She couldn't make out what either of them were saying, but she was fairly certain she had the gist of it. He was telling her aunt that Sarah was the only maid missing, no doubt.

After a few moments, her aunt's door was closed and the servant made his way back down the hall and took up his position near the main stairs again.

He'd been sent to catch her when she came out.

Poor Sarah.

Unsettled by the chaos she'd created, Demi moved back to her bed and climbed in, wondering if she had done the wrong thing by taking the coward's way out, despite Sarah's insistence. She knew Sarah was right in one respect, though. She couldn't help Sarah if she couldn't help herself, and Sarah had already taken the step of coming down. She would still have been in trouble, but possibly not nearly as much. She might have been able to think of a reasonable excuse for being downstairs in the middle of the night, or at least something that wouldn't get her instantly dismissed. Now she didn't have that option.

She was still wondering what Sarah would do when she heard a door open. Leaping from the bed, she raced across the room on tiptoe and planted her ear against the door panel.

"There ye are, ye brazen hussy! Lady Moreland left word yer to pack at once an' take yerself off."

"Did she?" Lord Wyndham said coolly. "Well, in that case, I think I should take myself off, as well. Have my carriage readied. I'll send my man around in the morning to collect my things."

"But … but, my lord! It's the middle of the night. The stablehands're all abed … and her ladyship won't be at all happy with this."

"Her happiness, of course, is my first concern," Garrett responded sardonically.

"I beg yer pardon, my lord. I only meant that her ladyship would not want ye ta feel as if ye must leave tonight."

"Nevertheless, as it happens, I find I'm far too eager to shake the dust of Moreland Abbey to wait for a more agreeable hour … and, in any case, I must see that Sarah is safely settled at the inn. I might just as well … enjoy the remainder of the night there."

The door was closed again. After a few moments, she heard Sarah and the manservant move off. Devastated, Demi turned and stared at her bed for several moments and finally moved across the room and climbed in.

She'd thought she was willing to face anything only to be with Garrett one last time before he vanished from her life forever, but she'd never expected anything even nearly as horrendous as what had happened. Not only had she succeeded in thoroughly disgusting Garrett of her, but she'd gotten Sarah discharged.

She was almost sorry she hadn't leapt from Garrett's window.

On the other hand, it seemed unlikely it would have ended things for her, or changed anything for the better for anyone else. Sarah had rushed to her rescue the moment she'd heard the commotion. Her aunt would probably still have blamed her for Demi's faults, probably would still have discharged her without a reference--and she would probably have ended up crippled, still married to Flemming, but no longer able to outrun him.

The only thing she could've done to help Sarah was not to have gone at all and, upon reflection, it had been disastrous all the way around. She wondered what had possessed her to say the things she had, to make Garrett think she was such a terrible person. She'd been angry and hurt, but that wasn't an excuse for adding stupidity to the situation. She supposed, maybe in the darkest part of her mind, she'd thought some of those things or it wouldn't have occurred to her to say them at all, but she hadn't done any of it for that reason, and now she'd never be able to convince Garrett that she hadn't. Even if he allowed her to explain, even if he accepted it because he wanted to, in the back of his mind that seed of doubt must always remain.

Sighing, she lay back against her pillows and pulled the covers up, trying to dredge up enough self pity to indulge in a good cry. Unfortunately, the magnitude of her transgressions was such that she was too shocked even to find that tiny refuge of relief. Eventually, however, exhaustion overwhelmed her.

Chapter Thirteen

The room was bright with light when the maid tapped at her door the following morning. Demi bolted upright in bed, certain at first that it was the summons from her aunt that she'd been more than half expecting from the moment she'd escaped detection the night before.

"I've brought a tray to break your fast," said a feminine voice from the other side of the panel that Demi didn't recognize.

She stared blankly at the door for several moments, trying to bring the blurred image into focus even while she worked on making sense of the confusion in her mind. Finally, she saw that she'd unbolted the door the night before and fell back onto her pillows, grateful she'd remembered to do so since it meant she didn't have to get out of bed. "Come!" she slurred sleepily, grabbing her coverlet and pulling it over her head as she rolled onto her side.

The night before crashed down upon her, driving sleep beyond her grasp as she listened disinterestedly to the maid's footsteps as she crossed the room and set the tray on the table near the bed. The smells of tea and fresh baked bread wafted to her. Instead of a welcome, familiar smell, it made her feel vaguely nauseated.

"Lady Moreland says to tell ye the seamstress is here for yer final fitting and not to keep her waiting too long. I can help ye dress if ye like, Miss Demitria."

Demi groaned. "I don't see much point in dressing if I'm to have the woman in here pulling it off directly," she muttered sullenly. "Just give me a few moments to wake up and she can come up."

"Yes, miss," the maid said and disappeared again.

When the door had closed, Demi flung off the covers and sat up. Her head was pounding, but that was hardly surprising given her activities the night before and the fact that she'd probably not slept more than four or five hours at the most. With an effort, she dragged herself from the bed and moved to the washstand to bathe.

She wondered as she did so what she was going to do about the maid's gown she'd filched from the laundry, and the damaged pantalets. Sarah would have helped her cover her transgressions, but Sarah was gone and she was completely on her own now.

In truth, she couldn't find that she cared a great deal any longer whether her aunt found out or not. She wasn't certain that she'd ever cared. She simply hadn't wanted to be discovered before she could do what she set out to do and afterwards she had been determined to make certain she wasn't discovered so that Garrett couldn't accuse her of having done it to trap him into marrying her. There was no longer much danger of that now that he was gone. In a few days, she knew she would be marrying Flemming, so it didn't seem to matter whether it was discovered after she'd left or not.

She finally set it aside, realizing that she wasn't in any state of mind to consider either the importance of covering her tracks or a plan to do so that might have some chance of success. When she finished bathing, she moved to the armoire and found a fresh pair of pantalets, stockings, and a chemise and sat down to dress herself. She couldn't put her corset on properly without help, but she donned it haphazardly, realizing the seamstress would no doubt want to adjust it anyway.

She was tying her garters when a knock came on her door once. Listlessly, she pulled her dressing gown over her shoulders and called out permission to enter. The seamstress, followed by her two assistants entered the room carrying several boxes. To her surprise, she had discovered the first time they'd come for a fitting that her aunt had actually commissioned two new day gowns and a walking dress besides the wedding gown.

Under the circumstances, she hadn't been terribly excited, even though it was the first time that she could remember actually getting gowns that had been made specifically for her. She tried to dredge up some pleasure as the women opened the boxes and displayed the finished gowns, but they had been designed with her position as the pastor's wife in mind and were far more serviceable and practical than lovely.

Nevertheless, when her aunt came in to observe the proceedings, she did her best to appear both resigned--which she was--and pleased--which she wasn't.

A wave of nausea washed over her again when the wedding gown was brought out. The dress was not to her taste, but she rather thought it was what the dress represented that caused her distress. Regardless, she said nothing, allowing them to push and pull and turn her once they had it on her and had adjusted it.

The dress didn't fit her particularly well she saw when she was allowed to study it in the mirror above her dressing table, but then, since everything she'd owned previously had been made for Phoebe, she wasn't accustomed to having gowns that fit particularly well anyway. When she'd looked it over long enough to appear at least a little interested, she turned away again.

"The veil," her aunt instructed, gesturing toward the one box remaining on her bed.

Demi's belly clenched and a feeling of uneasiness washed over her. Without a word, she sat on the bench and allowed one of the seamstress's assistants to comb and arrange her hair and then attach the cap and veil that went with the gown.

"There. Stand up and let me have a look at you."

Sighing, Demi stood and turned slowly so that her aunt could examine her. Finally, Alma Moreland nodded. "It will do. Thank you, Mrs. Sloan. You may go."

When the seamstress and her assistants had left, Lady Moreland fixed her with a look that brooked no argument. "Mr. Flemming is waiting at the church. Can I depend upon you to behave suitably? For I must tell you I have had quiet enough of your belligerence of late and I don't mean to deal with it today of all days. It's to be a quiet wedding, naturally, all things considered, but we must have witnesses."

The wave of nausea rushed back. "Today?" Demi asked faintly. "It's today?"

Lady Moreland shrugged. "You made it clear you had no interest in the proceedings. You can not complain now that you were not kept informed of the arrangements. Now, you can either comport yourself as the young lady I brought you up to be, or I can summon a couple of footmen and have your dosed with laudanum to assure us that you will be compliant. Which is it to be?"

As horrifying as the suggestion was, Demi felt an urge to request the laudanum. She rather relished the thought of being oblivious to what was happening. "You do not need to summon the footmen," she said quietly. "But ... perhaps a little laudanum ... just to settle my nerves?"

Lady Moreland eyed her suspiciously but finally nodded and moved to the door and grasped the bell pull, then hesitated and turned to look at Demi speculatively. "Come along to my room. I'd just as soon it wasn't common knowledge that you'd had to be sedated to go through with the wedding."

Meekly, Demi left the room and walked ahead of her aunt to her aunt's room. She'd never been in her aunt's room more than once or twice and once they were in the sitting room, she glanced around curiously as her aunt disappeared into her bedchamber. A few moments later, she reappeared with a small vial and held it out. "A capful, I should think, will be enough to settle your nerves."

Nodding, Demi took the vial and studied it for several moments. She'd never taken any, but she knew that both Lady Moreland and Phoebe dosed themselves with it whenever they were overwrought and unable to rest. Removing the lid with fingers that shook, she studied it a moment and finally put the bottle to her lips and turned it up, taking a long swallow. It tasted ghastly.

Before she could take another sip, her aunt slapped the bottle from her hand. "Are you out of your mind? You can not ... gulp it as if it were nothing but water! You will kill your fool self!"

Demi stared at her wide eyed. "I have taken too much?" she gasped, horrified.

Lady Moreland shook her head, though she looked distinctly unnerved as she picked up the bottle and examined it. "Most of it has spilled now. How am I to tell that, you wretched girl!"

Demi placed a hand over her stomach and one over her wildly fluttering heart. "Do you think I should try to bring it up?" she asked, feeling a cold fear wash over her with the realization that she'd swallowed something potentially fatal. Her aunt wasn't inclined to worry overmuch about her. If she was anxious, then Demi certainly felt that there was cause for alarm.

"And have you arrive at the church smelling as if you'd just been sick!" Lady Moreland snapped. Finally, she shook her head. "I'm sure it was not more than a swallow and you will be fine. You have only just broke your fast, so you've enough food in your stomach to make it safe enough, I feel certain."

Demi stared at her aunt wide-eyed, wondering if she should admit that she hadn't broken her fast. She'd felt too ill after the unsettling events the night before, and with lack of sleep, to feel up to tackling food so soon after she'd woken.

With an effort, she calmed herself. She'd taken no more than a sip. It could not be enough to truly hurt her, she felt certain, and if it affected her more powerfully because of her empty stomach, she wasn't convinced that was altogether a bad thing. Drawing in a calming breath, she nodded and followed her aunt from the room and down the corridor to the stairs.

A faint dizziness washed over her as she descended the stairs, but she assured herself it was merely nerves and lack of sleep. She'd only just taken the medicine. It could not effect her so quickly. She would be fortunate if it had calmed her nerves by the time they reached the church.

She discovered once they'd settle in the carriage, however, that she felt oddly peaceful for someone who was facing marriage with a dread not unlike someone facing the hangman. She even managed to smile at her cousin Phoebe when she settled beside her aunt.

"Are you all right, Demitria?" Phoebe asked her after a bit.

Demi dragged her gaze from the bizarre landscape they were passing and smiled at her cousin. "I think so. Yes."

"I gave her a bit of laudanum to settle her nerves," Lady Moreland volunteered.

Phoebe leaned forward, studying Demi's eyes.

Snickering, Demi leaned forward and put her nose to her cousin's.

Phoebe leaned back abruptly, frowning. "Do I look … like that, when I've had a dose of laudanum?" she asked in revulsion.

Lady Moreland frowned and Demi snickered again. "I told her only a capful. She took a great swallow instead, but no more than that. I expect it was a bit more than she should have had though, for she is not accustomed to taking it. We shall have to hurry or we'll end up having to hold her up to say her vows," she added irritably, and leaned forward to rap on the panel behind the driver. The panel slid open. "Faster, if you please."

The panel closed again and the carriage began to rock rather alarmingly … at least, Phoebe and Lady Moreland looked rather alarmed. Demi grasped the strap on the side of the carriage above her seat and chuckled as she stared out the window dreamily at the landscape, which had turned into a wild blur of colors. As suddenly as the carriage had picked up speed, however, it decreased so sharply that Phoebe and Lady Moreland nearly slid out of their seats. They released little yelps of surprise, which Demi found extremely funny, and then began to babble excitedly, wondering aloud what was happening as the carriage abruptly rocked to a shuddering halt.

The door was snatched open and Demi stared in surprise at Garrett. "Why, hallo, Garrett! You've come to see me married off to that great, hulking, prosy brute, Flemming?"

He frowned, his lips settling in a thin, tight line. "Nay. I've come to put a stop to this insanity. Come with me!"

Demi looked at him questioningly a moment but held out her hand readily. "Where are we going?"

"Now see here, my lord! You can not accost us on the king's highway in broad day light like a … a brigand, and spirit my niece off for your nefarious purposes!" Lady Moreland gasped in outrage, having found her voice at last.

"I already have," he said tightly. "Come, Demi. You'll not be marrying the pastor today … or any other day, for that matter."

"Don't even think, my girl! If you get out of this carriage, I wash my hands of you!"

Demi studied her aunt soberly for several moments. "I think it would be a relief, Aunt Alma."

"It won't be when he tires of you and casts you into the gutter with all the other harlots, mark my words! And he will, you little fool! Think before you do this foolish thing. You needn't think you can come crawling back to me when he discards you like an old shoe!"

Demi nodded. "I'll remember ... I'm not to come back. Good-bye, Cousin Phoebe," she said agreeably, allowing Garrett to help her from the carriage. When she'd gained the road and looked around, she saw that Garrett had a pistol trained on the driver. She looked at the pistol curiously and then at the driver. "You held up the carriage?"

Garrett gave her a piercing look but returned his attention to the driver, motioning with the barrel of the gun for the driver to set the horses in motion once more.

Demi turned to wave at her aunt and cousin. Lady Moreland, her nose in the air, was staring angrily at the seat across from her and didn't even bother to glance her way. Phoebe was staring at both Demi and Garrett as if they had grown two heads. Shrugging, Demi turned back to Garrett, watching as he slipped his pistol into his saddle bag. When he'd fastened it, he turned to her, caught her around the waist, and then lifted her up and settled her on the front of his saddle. She grasped a fistful of the horse's mane as he climbed up behind her. When he slipped an arm around her waist to steady her, she settled back against him trustingly, her lips curling in a smile.

"Fitzhugh is to meet us on the Bath road. We'll save time if we cut across country. I don't expect Flemming to try anything, but I'll feel better when I have you safely away from here."

Demi frowned, trying to decide whether she was particularly worried about it and finally decided that she wasn't. She couldn't seem to feel much of anything beyond a glorious sense of relief that she wasn't going to have to marry Jonathan Flemming after all. Nodding, she stroked Garrett's thigh lovingly for deciding to take her as his mistress after all, despite the awful things she'd said, after she'd nearly gotten him into trouble the night before.

His hand tightened on her waist as he turned the horse and kicked it into a trot. It moved along the road for a short distance, then gathered itself and jumped the hedgerow at the side of the road. The jolt when they landed on the other side snapped Demi's teeth together. Her head swum dizzily, making concentration difficult.

She realized though that she was in Garrett's arms and that was just the place she wanted to be. Now he was hers … for as long as it lasted, but she didn't want to think about that. He was hers for now. He wanted her. He would take her far away from her aunt and make love to her any time she wanted him to.

It was a heady thought, and sent a spiral of warmth through her, making the muscles low in her belly clench in excitement and anticipation. After a moment, she pulled his hand from her waist and pushed it downward, cupping it against her femininity through her clothes. He stiffened slightly, but after a moment, his hand cupped her tightly, his fingers stroking her.

Heat surged through her. The motion of his hands, and the movements of the horse beneath them reminded her of their lovemaking. Need began to thrum through her veins and the cloth became a nuisance, preventing her from enjoying his caress. Gathering her skirts, she pulled them out of the way and guided his hand to the slit in the crotch of her pantalets. A groan escaped her as she felt his touch on the tiny nub of flesh just above her woman's place.

She stroked his thighs as he stroked her and finally reached behind and between them to rub the erect member she felt digging into her back, stroking him through his breeches as he'd stroked her through her skirts. She felt his heated breath against her cheek a moment before he spoke.

"As much as I'd like to accommodate you, this is not the time, my dear," he growled against her ear.

"We needn't stop," she gasped a little desperately. "Only let me touch you as you touch me."

He groaned. After a moment, however, he released her

and unfastened his breeches and she slipped her hand around his heated length, stroking him as he slipped his arm around her again and began to stroke her once more. His breath became as ragged as her own. Finally, he pulled back on the reins. When the horse stopped, he pulled her hand from his flesh and Demi twisted around to give him a look of reproach. His lips twisted. "This is more insane, if at all possible, than holding up your aunt's coach," he growled, catching her face with one hand and leaning down to kiss her deeply.

Demi kissed him back fervently, struggling to turn in the restricted space and face him. He tightened his arms around her, lifting her slightly so that she could turn to meet him fully and Demi wrapped her legs around his waist, pressing herself tightly against him. The horse sidled beneath them, jogging forward a couple of steps and he pulled back on the reins once more.

Only peripherally aware of anything beyond the feel of Garrett against her and the heat surging through her as he kissed her, Demi shifted until she felt his erection slide along her cleft teasingly. She arched her hips, moving against him as she kissed him back with equal fervor, following him as he withdrew his tongue from her mouth and exploring his mouth as he'd caressed hers. He groaned. Reaching down, he lifted her hips slightly and aligned his own body with hers, rocking his hips until his erection began to slip inside of her inch by excruciating inch.

At last, he plumbed her depths and a sense of triumph filtered through Demi's heat fogged mind as pleasure radiated outward from the intimate caress. Tightening her thighs, she lifted upward slightly and then settled down on his lap again. Abruptly, the horse jogged forward again. This time, however, instead of pulling it to a halt, Garrett allowed it to break into a fast walk and the horse's gait bounced them gently against each other, sending out shards of glorious sensation with each grinding contact of their bodies.

Demi wanted it to go on forever, but within moments, she felt her body tensing toward completion. Groaning, she moved a little faster. As if her voice or her movements encouraged the horse, it began to move a little more quickly, jouncing them together harder and faster so that his manhood stroked her faster, harder, deeper each time they came together. Demi cried out abruptly as the pleasure built to a crescendo and crashed explosively through her. Garrett's arms tightened around her, pulling the horse to a stop as he convulsed with pleasure moments behind her.

Demi lay weakly against him, feeling wonderfully sated and vaguely pleased with herself. Dimly, she realized that at least a part of her satisfaction was that she'd provoked him into making love to her when he'd been reluctant to do so, but part, she knew was also because she couldn't believe he would soon grow tired of her if she inspired his lust to the point where he threw caution to the wind as he just had … in the open where they might be seen, on the back of a horse.

Almost as if he'd read her mind, he muttered, "That was more than a little insane."

Demi snuggled closer, feeling herself sinking toward sleep. "It felt wonderful, though," she murmured groggily.

His arms tightened around her briefly, but then he gently disentangled himself from her, reaching between them to adjust his clothing. Demi made a half hearted attempt to adjust her own clothing, but she found that she was so sleepy she really didn't care. She could hardly keep her eyes open or hold her head upright. It seemed far too heavy for her neck.

Garrett gave her a little shake and finally grasped her jaw, tilting her face up. She managed a faint smile but found she couldn't lift her eyelids. Garrett pried one eyelid up with his thumb. It jolted her enough that she drew back, looking at him questioningly. "What's wrong with you?" he asked harshly.

Demi smiled. "Nothing, my lord. I'm just a little sleepy."

He shook her. "Demi, wake up!"

She opened her eyes again.

"What did you take?"

She frowned, thinking it over. "Just a little laudanum," she said finally, surprised to discover her words were as slurred as if she'd been drinking strong spirits. "Aunt

Alma said it would relax me."

"Christ! I should have known." He shook her again. "How much did you take?"

"Doan know … big gulp."

"Right out of the bottle? Did you dilute it?"

"Nope."

Dismounting abruptly, he dragged her off the horse and slowly lowered her until she was kneeling on the ground. "You've had too much. You need to expel what you can."

Demi looked at him in confusion. "Can't spit it out. Done drank it."

He shook her again, harder this time. "Run your finger down your throat, or I will."

She glared at him. "I don't want to be sick. I want to sleep."

"That's what I'm afraid of," he ground out, prying her jaws apart and running his finger down her throat. Gagging, she retched into the grass until she could retch no more. Somewhere in the rounds, the desperate need to sleep began to dissipate slightly. She was aware enough, at any rate, to realize she'd had quite enough.

When Garrett caught her jaw once more, she opened her eyes wide. "Not sleepy anymore," she lied.

He studied her eyes grimly for several moments, but apparently he was satisfied. After a moment, he pulled his handkerchief from his pocket and handed it to her. She took it, sitting back on her heels as she wiped her mouth. Moving back to the horse, he pulled the flask from his saddle bag that he'd handed her once before and strode back to her.

Pulling the top off, he held it to her lips. "Don't swallow it. Just rinse your mouth with it. Understand?"

She nodded and did as he told her. Finally, he helped her to her feet, lifted her and settled her on the horse again. With an effort, she held on until he was mounted behind her. Cursing again, he pulled the veil from her hair and tossed it to the ground. "Don't go to sleep, sweetheart. Talk to me."

Nodding meekly, she cast around in her mind for something to say. Nothing came immediately to mind, however. "About what?"

"Anything," he said grimly, pulling her tightly against him and urging the horse into motion once more.

"I'm sorry about last night," she said finally. "I didn't mean ... any of that."

"None of it?" he asked absently.

She frowned, thinking it over. "I wanted you to make love to me," she said finally. "You didn't, though, did you?"

His arm tightened around her. "I'd as soon not talk about all of the incredibly stupid things I've said and done since we met, love. We'll sort that out another time. Suffice to say Sarah gave me a good dressing down and brought me to my senses in time to prevent complete disaster."

Demi twisted around to look at him. "Sarah?"

Smiling faintly, he lifted his hand from her waist long enough to caress her cheek briefly. "Aye, Sarah."

Demi thought it over. Something had been nagging at her since the night before when she'd listened at the door to the conversation between Lord Wyndham and the servant. "You did not ... share your bed with Sarah?"

He looked taken aback. "Good God! I should think not!" A worried frown marred his brow in the next moment. "The opium in the laudanum ... don't allow that to take hold of your mind, love. The answer is most definitely not. I arranged *another* room for her at the inn. She did not sleep in my room and certainly not in my bed.

"She's a handsome woman, I'll warrant you that, but I've no eyes ... and no desire, for anyone but you. I would think that would be abundantly clear to you by now, love."

Chapter Fourteen

Garrett kept her talking for hours it seemed. They reached the Bath road eventually and rode along it for several miles before they came upon Garrett's coach. Garrett dismounted, tied the reins to the back of the coach and finally helped her from the horse. Holding her arm and walking her around to the side of the coach, he helped her to climb in, then followed her inside. Fitzhugh gave Garrett a disapproving look as he closed the door. "I thought you would ride along side, my lord."

Garrett frowned. "Her aunt dosed her with laudanum to make certain she was ... not difficult. I'll stay with her for a bit, at least until I'm convinced she's past the worst of it."

"Very good, sir," Fitzhugh said at once and turned away, climbing up beside the driver.

"I'm fine," Demi assured him.

"Still sleepy?"

She bit her lip. "Only a little ... but I did not sleep much last night," she reminded him.

"Indulge me, then."

Smiling, Demi leaned toward him as the coach lurched into motion and walked her fingers up his chest teasingly. "Gladly."

He caught her hand, but he chuckled. "As happily as I would accept that particular form of indulgence, I've been told I must be on my best behavior by both Fitzhugh and Sarah. And I can well imagine my mother would vociferously second them. I can not allow you to lead me into further temptation ... at the moment. Particularly since I'm well aware you're still suffering the effects of the drug you took.

"That was not at all wise of you, love. What possessed you to take so much?"

Demi settled her cheek against his shoulder. "Aunt Alma said she would summon the footmen and make me take it if I was determined to be difficult. I knew she and Phoebe had taken it often enough for their nerves. I only thought that it would relax me, so I wouldn't be so afra--nervous."

Garrett relaxed fractionally. "I'm relieved to hear it was no more than an oversight. You are most unfortunately accident prone, love. I can see I will have to keep my eye on you," he said pensively. "As for your aunt ... as much as it grieves me, I'm afraid there is little I can do in retaliation for what she put you through."

When they stopped at the first post, he sent Fitzhugh into the inn to procure a light luncheon in a basket for them. Demi thought it strange at first that they ate in the coach, but she said nothing, finally realizing that it was the impropriety of their situation. It hardly seemed to matter now. She felt certain she was the most scandalous of fallen women in all of England by now, but she didn't particularly wish to be stared at, nor publicly shunned either.

She wasn't particularly hungry, despite the fact that she hadn't eaten since she'd risen, but she ate a little at Garrett's insistence. The food only seemed to make her more sleepy rather than less so, but to her relief, Garrett held her close and at last allowed her to sleep.

It was dark when she awoke. She stirred sleepily, confused by the rocking of the coach and the hardness of her bed. Finally, she realized that Garrett had dragged her across his lap, cradling her head against his shoulder. She tipped her head back, placing a light kiss along his jaw.

"Feeling better?" he asked.

The moment she moved, her head had begun to pound as if someone was hammering on her skull. "Yes," she lied, but groaned as he shifted, settling her on the seat beside him and leaning forward to stretch his cramped muscles. "My head hurts, though."

"I would be surprised if it didn't," he muttered. "In the future, you will avoid laudanum, my dear."

Demi massaged her throbbing temples. "I will certainly not be tempted to repeat the experience if it's to have this effect, I can assure you."

"Good." Leaning forward, he tapped on the panel. It slid open at once. "I believe I'll get out and ride a bit."

"Very good, sir. We've reached the park."

"Good timing," Garrett commented as he sat back and looked over at Demi.

"You're getting out?" Demi asked in dismay as the coach slowed and finally came to a halt.

He patted her cheek and climbed down. "We're almost home."

Demi frowned as she settled back against the seat cushions and the coach lurched into motion once more, wondering where 'home' was. In truth, she couldn't remember more than snatches of the conversation they'd had since he'd pulled her from her aunt's carriage, but she didn't think they had discussed where they were going.

She did remember being ill, unfortunately. She covered her face with her hands, mortified both by that memory, and remembrance of what she'd done directly before she'd been sick.

Lord! Garrett must think she was-- She broke that thought off. Of course, he thought she was a completely wanton slut! What else could he think after the way she'd fallen all over herself to spread her legs for him any time he touched her.

Possibly the worst of it was that only thinking about making love to him on the back of his horse made her feel warm all over again, in a purely carnal sense, not from shame, as it should have been.

She was incorrigible--beyond redemption.

It occurred to her, however, that perhaps that was what drew Garrett to her. Maybe he'd sensed that in her all along? Even though she hadn't really known or understood the particulars regarding intimacy between a man and woman, she realized now that she had lusted for him the moment she'd set eyes on him. It was indeed love, as she believed, but far more than mere affection, respect, liking. Only looking at him had been enough to make her heart run away from her, to steal her breath, send warmth and need spiraling through her.

And from the moment he'd touched her, she'd grown blind and deaf to everything she'd ever been taught about respectable, acceptable behavior.

What *could* he think except that she was mad for him and perfectly happy to damn the world if only she could be with him?

And what was to become of her now? Would he hide her away in a little cottage somewhere and come to her only when the whim struck him?

How could he do anything else? She was disgraced. However much he might enjoy being with her, he could not be seen in public with her. He could not have her in his home. Society would not stand for such a blatant scandalous display and he would have to marry eventually, if for no other reason than to secure an heir.

As unclear as her memory was, however, of all that had happened since she'd decided to take the laudanum to settle her nerves, she remembered the most pertinent parts--Her aunt had disowned her. The thought didn't particularly wound her, but it frightened her.

What *would* she do when Garrett tired of her? She knew, sooner or later, that he was bound to, and just as surely, he would discard her and look for a new mistress. Men always did. Would she be passed from one to another? Or would he be kind enough to buy that little cottage he'd once offered her?

The slowing of the coach distracted her from her morbid thoughts. She glanced out of the window, but it was far too dark by now to see since the moon hadn't risen above the trees as yet. She saw light before the coach, but she couldn't tell if it was only the carriage lamps or if they were approaching the lights of a house.

She settled back again, nervously checking her hair and clothing as she felt the coach lurch and begin to bounce along cobbles. Her heart leapt into her throat and lodged itself there as the coach drew up before an enormous mansion. Torches were lit on either side of the main door, throwing a flickering light over much of the exterior. Inside, the light of many candles lit the windows that faced the drive.

Before she could recover her composure, the door opened and the steps were let down. Garrett, looking tired and drawn stood in the opening, holding his hand out to her. After a moment, Demi took it and allowed him to help her down. As they ascended the steps, the door to the manor opened abruptly and an attractive woman wearing a scandalously thin gown of the first stare of fashion seemed to float effortlessly down toward them. "You must be Miss Demitria Standish. Welcome to Wyndham Park, my dear."

Demi glanced uncertainly at Lord Wyndham and then back at the woman once more. Finally, remembering her manners, she curtsied. "Thank you."

The woman chuckled at her look of confusion, holding out her hand. "I'm Lady Wyndham."

Demi felt the blood rush from her face. A wave of dizziness followed it.

"Goodness! You poor little thing. You're all done in, aren't you. You must come in at once and let me get you settled. I've arranged for you to have the blue room. Garrett, be a dear and see to her baggage," she said distractedly.

Demi glanced a little fearfully at Garrett as the woman slipped an arm around her waist and led her inside. He was frowning. She could tell nothing from his expression, however.

She didn't have time to consider it. They paused only briefly in the foyer, where Lady Wyndham issued orders to scurrying servants like a general situating his troops, and then she was led up the stairs. Servants were summoned to prepare a bath. By the time they reached the upper landing, two footman had struggled in through the front door, carrying a large trunk between them. Demi, drawn by the commotion, glanced down at the men, feeling the strange sense of being disconnected with her surroundings that is typical of dreams. She stared at the trunk curiously and without recognition, wondering why Garrett hadn't told Lady Wyndham that she had no trunk ... nothing to her name beyond the clothing she was standing in.

She was too stunned to think beyond a specific point-- Garrett had brought her to his home and handed her over to Lady Wyndham for some unfathomable reason. She was led into a small chamber where a tub had already been prepared, helped to undress, and assisted into the tub.

"There now, my dear. That should set you to rights in no time at all. I've always found a nice hot bath very soothing to the nerves, and I've only to look at you to see you've had a very trying day. Would you prefer to dine in the dining room? Or should I have a tray prepared for you?"

Demi stared at her blankly for several moments, revolted at the thought of sitting down to dine at Lady Wyndham's table. "I'm not really hungry," she said tentatively.

Lady Wyndham's brows rose. "You have eaten already?"

Demi blushed. "We … uh … stopped for luncheon."

Lady Wyndham patted her on the cheek. "I will have a tray sent up. I can see you're not feeling up to company just now. And when you're settled, perhaps we'll have a little chat?"

Demi found when Lady Wyndham left that she'd been right. The hot bath went a long way toward relaxing her and reviving her flagging spirits. Some of the sense of drifting through a dream, or perhaps a nightmare, also dissipated, but the uneasiness of confusion lingered. What position, she wondered, was she to have in Lord Wyndham's home? Why had he brought her here? He could not, surely, expect to house his wife and his mistress in the same place.

She assumed Lady Wyndham was his wife. She looked to be several years Garrett's senior, but she certainly didn't appear to be old enough to be his mother.

Finally, deciding she simply wasn't up to dealing with anything more at the moment, she concentrated on her bath. When she'd finished washing her hair, one of the maid's helped her rinse the soap from it and then wrung the excess water from it and twisted a length of linen around her head. The soap given her to bathe with was scented with roses and smelled divine. She lingered over her bath until her skin began to prune and finally, reluctantly, stood up and took the length of toweling the maid handed her. To her surprise, the maid disappeared for several moments and returned with her own clothing and helped her dress.

Apparently the trunk that had been brought up actually had been her trunk, but the when and how of it stymied her. Obviously, Lady Moreland had had her things packed up in anticipation of moving them to the parsonage after the wedding, but how had the trunk ended in Garrett's hands?

Had it already been loaded into Lady Moreland's carriage? Or had Fitzhugh, perhaps, waylaid the servants' carriage as Garrett waylaid her aunt's?

Shaking it off as unanswerable, Demi followed the maid into the bedchamber that adjoined the small room where she'd bathed. It was an enormous room--far bigger than the room that had been hers at Moreland Abbey, and far more richly appointed.

A large mahogany bed, in the Empire style, dominated the room, its canopy, hangings and coverlet all predominately blue. Two large carpets covered much of the gleaming wooden floor and these were also picked out in a similar shade of powder blue. A full length mirror was set in one corner and angled so that it caught much of the room in its reflection. Opposite the mirror was an enormous armoire, also of the Empire style. A maid was kneeling before it, busily unpacking the trunk that had been brought up and placing her clothing inside the cabinet in careful order.

Along the wall between the armoire and the mirror was a huge fireplace. A small, but cheerful little fire had been built on the hearth, despite the fact that it was already well into spring and the room was only a little chilled from the night air.

Feeling her tension of before return, Demi removed the linen from her head and moved to stand before the fire to allow the heat to dry her hair, surreptitiously studying the remainder of the room as the maid who'd assisted her with her bath went to retrieve a chemise and pantalets from her trunk.

Two windows, easily twice her height, lined the wall on either side of the massive head board of the bed, swathed in heavy draperies of a solid blue slightly darker than the carpets. Along the wall opposite her was a long dressing table with a padded bench and a large mirror above it. Just beyond that was the door she'd

entered through and in the corner of the inner wall--
which led, she surmised, to the upper hallway--was an
arrangement of two overstuffed chairs and several small
tables. A long bench was situated at the foot of the
massive bed and, near the hearth where she stood, a set
of two comfortably overstuffed chairs with a small table
between them.

It looked like the sort of apartment one might set aside
for visiting royalty, not the sort of room reserved for
unwelcome guests of no social standing who also
happened to be poverty stricken orphans, and certainly
not a man's mistress.

"Would you prefer to dress? Or prepare for bed, Miss
Demitria?" the maid asked when she'd helped Demi
don her pantalets and chemise.

Demi looked at her uncertainly. "Didn't Lady
Wyndham say she wished to speak to me? I think I
should get dressed to receive her."

The maid nodded and returned a few moments later
with a corset, which she helped Demi into and adjusted.
"Which gown do you prefer, Miss?"

Demi shook her head. "Whatever you think."

The maid brought one of the gowns her aunt had had
made up for her marriage. Demi stared at it in revulsion,
but she knew her other gowns looked the worse for
wear and she didn't particularly want to greet Lady
Wyndham in her castoffs.

The maid was just finishing when, after a quick rap on
the door, Lady Wyndham entered, followed by a maid
carrying a tray. The dinner was set up on the small table
in the corner and, with some reluctance, Demi joined
Lady Wyndham there, perching uncomfortably on the
edge of the chair opposite the one Lady Wyndham had
taken.

Once they'd been served, Lady Wyndham shooed the
servants out.

"Now that we are quite alone, you must tell me all
about yourself and my son. When are you to be
married? I confess I have my heart set upon a very
large, elaborate affair, but since it is your wedding, I
suppose we will do it up however you prefer."

Demi stared at her blankly for several moments while

it slowly sank into her mind that Lady Wyndham was not, as she'd feared, Garrett's wife, but his mother.

And she thought they were being married.

Blood flooded her cheeks. As reluctant as she was to confess the situation to his mother, of all people, she knew she simply could not deal with any more subterfuge. "I don't … that is, he hasn't asked me to marry him, Lady Wyndham. I am … quite convinced he has no intention, or at least no desire, to do so," she confessed weakly and then covered her face and promptly burst into tears.

Chapter Fifteen

To Demi's stunned amazement, Lady Wyndham pulled her into a motherly embrace, rocking her slightly and patting her back. "There, there, my dear. It can not, surely, be as bad as all that?"

The embrace and the soothing words only made her wail harder. Or perhaps it was only that she couldn't even recall a time when she had been comforted by the loving embrace of a mother. It occurred to her after a bit, however, that it was not her own mother who comforted her, but Garrett's. With an effort, she regained control of her wayward emotions and began a frantic search for her handkerchief. Finding it at last, she pulled away from Lady Wyndham and mopped her face and blew her nose.

Lady Wyndham sat back on her heels. After a moment, she rose and moved back to her own seat. When Demi finally nerved herself to look at the older woman, she saw that her face was a mask of carefully controlled anger. It sent a shaft of fear through her, effectively dashing the last of her urge to cry.

"But ... this is infamous! Outrageous!"

Feeling the blood rush from her face, Demi stood abruptly. "I should go," she said a little desperately, uncertain of where she might go, but feeling a great urge to remove herself from Wyndham Park as quickly as possible.

Lady Wyndham gaped at her. "I beg your pardon?"

"I do apologize for ... for intruding on your hospitality. I didn't realize that he was bringing me here or I would have objected."

Understanding dawned. "No, no! You misunderstood me, my dear. I meant it was infamous of my son! I certainly do not consider *you* at fault. In any case, it is not my hospitality, precisely. Wyndham Park is Garrett's seat. But never mind that now. It's of no consequence.

"Do you mean to tell me that my son has seduced you ... a young lady of good family ... and carried you off without even having the grace to ask you to marry him?"

Demi stared a Lady Wyndham in horror, wishing the floor would open and swallow her. She couldn't allow Garrett to be blamed for her bad behavior, however. "It was not like that," she finally managed to say although she thought/hoped for several moments that she might simply faint dead away and be spared having to actually admit her transgressions aloud ... to Garrett's mother. "I ... uh ... I seduced him."

Lady Wyndham stared at her blankly for several moments. A chuckle escaped her and she clapped a hand to her mouth. When she removed her hand to speak, however, she began to giggle almost uncontrollably. "You seduced...." She fought another round with her mirth. "I'm sorry, child. Truly, I am. I realize this is very difficult for you. It's only ... darling you can not be unaware of the fact that Garrett has the reputation of being a dreadful rake!"

Demi reddened. "He does not have so bad a reputation as that!"

Lady Wyndham bit her lip. "You are right. It's unconscionable for me to blacken my own son's name. He is not a very notorious rake, not considered beyond the pale, but he is most certainly considered a rake, nevertheless."

Demi studied her for several moments and finally looked down at her hands. "I had heard a few things, I confess, but I could not credit it. He has always behaved in a most gentlemanly way toward me."

"Except when he seduced you," Lady Wyndham put in dryly.

Demi reddened, refusing to look up. "But he didn't. He'd been injured, you see. My cousin Geoffrey is quiet notoriously dangerous with a gun. They'd gone out shooting and he managed to fall from his horse and shoot Gar--Lord Wyndham in the ... in the leg. And he was very, very ill. He almost died and I was worried sick. So ... I sneaked into his room ... just to reassure myself that he would be all right, I swear. But then, he mistook me for a maid and ... and ... it just happened."

She flicked a look at Lady Wyndham and saw she was studying her skeptically. "He was in his cups," she added.

"And unable to recognize you? How convenient for him!"

Demi remembered abruptly that he'd admitted that he had recognized her and she shifted uncomfortably. "He was not himself," she insisted stubbornly. "He would have stopped if I'd asked him to. I ... didn't. So, it was all my fault, you see."

"No. I'm afraid I don't see. In any case, if he has compromised you in such a way, then he will most certainly marry you!"

Demi stared at her in dismay. "But that is just it! He ... he thinks I only did it so that he would be forced to marry me. And I didn't. I swear I didn't. But I simply could not *bear* it if he were forced to marry me. He would hate me and I'd rather die, really I would. Couldn't you ... just let me work for you ... or something? I could be a very good lady's maid, I think." She studied Lady Wyndham's expression for a moment and revised that. "Or a kitchen maid. I'm sure I could learn it very quickly."

Lady Wyndham frowned. "Wouldn't you rather have your pastor than be a scullery maid?"

Demi felt the blood rush from her face. She shuddered. "No! Please don't send me back to him. I'll leave ... in the morning. Or, now."

Lady Wyndham's brows rose. "And go where, child? Your aunt will almost certainly have disowned you. You have no other family? No friends who might take you in?"

"Sarah!" Demi said. "I'm sure Sarah wouldn't mind if I stayed with her a bit--just until I had time to figure out what to do."

"The new lady's maid who arrived this morning?"

"Oh," Demi said, deflated.

Lady Wyndham shook her head and reached over to pat Demi on the knee. "You are distressing yourself needlessly. I will sort through this. In the meanwhile, you must eat your dinner like a good girl and then rest. I will have something worked out very shortly, I can assure you, so you may be easy."

Food was the last thing Demi wanted at the moment. Her stomach was tied in knots, but she was somewhat relieved by Lady Wyndham's offer to straighten things out for her and she didn't want to appear ungrateful. She managed to eat enough to satisfy her and finally climbed into bed. To her surprise, Lady Wyndham tucked her in and kissed her on the forehead before she left, a militant gleam in her eyes.

She found Garrett pacing the library, a tumbler of scotch in his hand. Eyeing the glass with disfavor, she settled herself on the settee in front of the fireplace and watched him for several moments. Finally Garrett sprawled in the chair opposite her, rubbing his throbbing leg absently. "What do you think of her mother?"

Lady Wyndham frowned. "She's a darling girl … and far too good for you."

Garrett winced. "As it happens, I agree."

Slightly mollified, Lady Wyndham turned to study the fire. "Dearest, I beg you to come at once to Wyndham to attend my bride. I have made the most damnable mess of things," she quoted the note she'd received from him thoughtfully. "I'll admit, I could hardly credit it, but I had not thought you were sincere."

His dark brows rose. A faint smile curled his lips. "About my bride?"

Her lips thinned in irritation. "About the damnable mess, Garrett. She will not marry you."

To her surprise, he turned perfectly white. Standing abruptly, he moved to the window, staring out at the darkness beyond. "She has said that?"

Lady Wyndham studied his back for several moments. "I can not recall her precise words but it was something to the effect that 'she'd rather die'."

Garrett's head snapped around, his expression completely unguarded for once in his life, and eloquent of pained surprise. A moment later, a cold mask replaced it. "She is … distraught. Given time she will see that it's inevitable."

Despite her empathy for his suffering, and her

certainty that her son had at last succumbed to cupid's bow, his arrogant dismissal of Demitria's objections irritated her. So far as she could see, he *had* made a damnable mess of things. It was obvious to her that Demitria was deeply in love with him as he was with her, and yet he'd allowed her to feel as if he didn't return her affection, that he was willing to 'do the right thing' by her when, in fact, it had nothing to do with his wish to marry the girl, beyond conveniently tying things up for him.

For her son's sake, for Demitria's sake, she could not allow it. Despite the love they felt for one another, they could not begin a life together built on such a misunderstanding and expect to find happiness. In the back of Demitria's mind she would always believe that he had only married her because he felt honor bound to do so, perhaps even Garrett would have some doubts and it would destroy their happiness.

She frowned but didn't comment on his remark. After a few moments, he paced from the window to the fireplace and turned to face her. "I could hardly credit it, but she says you didn't even ask her to marry you," she said tentatively.

He flushed. "The moment did not seem … opportune. I intended, naturally, to formally request her hand," he said stiffly.

Lady Wyndham resisted the urge to roll her eyes. An untimely amusement flooded her, however, to see her son behave so awkwardly. He was generally so self-possessed, so urbane. She found it difficult to conceive that he had so lost his head that he had behaved like a green boy--even to stealing his bride at the end of a pistol!

"Well," she finally said decisively. "You will have plenty of time to mull it over and watch for the perfect opportunity. I have decided that I will take her with me to town. I expect most everyone has departed for the country by now, but there will be a few lingering in town and it will give me the opportunity to repair a little of the damage you two have done between you. I will scotch whatever rumors I can and see to having a decent wardrobe for her.

"In the meanwhile, you may cool your heels here, my son, and consider how badly you have handled everything. If you wish to marry her, you will have to consider wooing her. She most certainly deserves to be properly courted and I expect no less from you."

Garrett studied her uncomfortably. "As much as I appreciate your efforts, mother, I feel I should point out that there is a possibility that she is with child, in which case it will not do to put things off indefinitely, or even for very long. I should see to the posting of the banns....."

Lady Wyndham gaped at him indignantly. "Have you heard nothing I've said? Really, Garrett! You were not used to be so dense! She will not have you, and until or unless you convince her to change her mind, we will not make arrangements for a wedding."

Garrett's eyes narrowed dangerously. "I've admitted my error. I am willing to make amends, but I can not guard her reputation if you are to have her gallivanting about until it is obvious that she's with child."

Lady Wyndham glared back at him. Rising from the settee, she stalked across the room and poked his chest with her index finger. "You are willing," she said angrily. "You have compromised her and now you will condescend to marry her?"

He flushed. "I am very willing," he said between clenched teeth.

"You are very much a dolt!" Lady Wyndham snapped. "And more a fool than I would ever have believed. She loves you--stupidly, I must say, for I've no idea at all how she could have come to."

Garrett's expression softened instantly. "She told you that?"

Lady Wyndham's eyes narrowed. "She has not told you that, though, has she?"

He frowned, obviously thinking hard.

"Nor you her?"

He reddened. "That is not your affair," he said coolly.

Lady Wyndham shook her head. "Garrett, you must see that it would ruin everything for you to marry her, allowing her to believe that you have been forced into it?"

"I am honor bound--" he began stiffly.

"To be a complete fool, apparently," his mother snapped. "Have it your way! But if you can not win her as you should, then I will have no part in arranging a wedding! I will gladly take her under my wing. I will do whatever I can to repair the damage to her reputation, but I will not encourage her to marry you or insist upon it. You must muddle through that on your own."

Garrett stared at the vibrating door panel when his mother had left, slamming it behind her, wondering what had come over her. She was, in general, not the least volatile and to be depended upon for her practical, straightforward approach to things.

Settling in his chair, he stared pensively at the fire on the hearth, trying to figure out what it was that his mother had been so furious about. He would have thought that she would be furious with him for seducing Demi if anything, and angry with him if he had not decided that he should marry her.

Why would she be willing to aid and abet Demi's decision *not* to marry him?

For that matter, he could not fathom why Demi would object to marrying him. She'd given herself to him willingly--more than that, enthusiastically. She must feel something for him. His mother seemed convinced that she loved him, so why the theatrics about preferring death to marriage to him, he wondered angrily.

The proposal itself was merely a formality. He knew women set great store by such things, but it was inconceivable that she could love him, give herself to him, and then refuse to marry him only because he hadn't gotten down on one knee and requested her hand.

He studied the scotch in his glass suspiciously for several moments, but he was certain he hadn't drank enough to account for the fact that nothing that had just happened made any sense to him.

Sighing, he set the tumbler down and rubbed his temples irritably. Demi had scared him out of a good ten years of life today, he felt certain. First off, he'd arrived at Moreland Abbey to demand her aunt hand her over, only to discover the damned woman had snatched

Demi from beneath his nose and taken off for the church with her. Then, having chased her down and been forced to hold up the carriage like a brigand, or a common thief, he'd discovered the silly chit had over dosed herself on laudanum.

The desperation to find a doctor, rather than fleeing with his stolen bride, had been nearly overwhelming, but he'd realized there was nothing anyone could do for her. She would either live through it, or not. For hours he'd lived in the worst dread imaginable, shaking her awake every time she tried to succumb completely to the lure of the opium, sorely tempted for the first time in his life to throttle a woman.

His fingers flexed as he thought of her aunt and he had to consciously force them to relax. Abruptly, he got up and poured himself another scotch, deciding that he would find the right moment on the morrow and propose to Demi, so that she could be in no doubt at all that he was completely serious about honoring his obligations to her.

To his rage, and complete chagrin, however, he discovered when he returned from his morning ride that his mother had packed Demi off to London.

Chapter Sixteen

As uncomfortable as Demi was with the situation she found herself in, she discovered that it was impossible to remain that way. Lady Wyndham introduced her everywhere they went as her 'dear young friend' who was practically a daughter to her and hinted that she would be very happy to claim her as one. That part made her uncomfortable, but Lady Wyndham assured her she was not to worry her head about it, that she would be perfectly content for things to remain as they were until such time as Demi decided what she would do. She also pointed out that Demi needn't feel as if she was duty bound to accept Garrett, whatever had transpired between them.

That suggestion made her even more uncomfortable, but since Lady Wyndham made it clear that she was determined to arrange a match for her, Demi found herself being courted, much to her surprise, by several young men who seemed completely aware that her circumstances did not make her a great catch, and who seemed not to care that she was an orphan with no expectations.

Of course, she was certain they were not aware that she was not, by any stretch of the imagination, pure, but the Regent's set, of which Lady Wyndham was a part of, was a bit more wild than sedate and not nearly as concerned about propriety as her aunt had been. Many flaunted lovers openly. Of course, these were older women, and primarily widows, but even the young women tended to be racy.

As Demi had dreaded, she was confronted about the rumors regarding her carriage ride with Mr. Flemming. Lady Wyndham merely laughed and waved it away. "Oh heavens! That does sound deliciously wicked, I know, but it was not at all like that, I assure you! Why, the entire town knows that his sixteen year old daughter accompanied them, and I simply can not imagine any man playing at hanky panky in front of his impressionable daughter! No, no! Miss Wynthrope is far too quick to judge others by her own manners. It was only that the man took the notion to race his carriage home and nearly over set them ... but, there you are. Men are always completely convinced that they are much better at everything than they actually are. And my dear Miss Standish was so unsettled by the experience that she called the entire engagement off right then and there. As well she should have, for you must know if a man has reached the age of thirty and five and has no more common sense than that, it isn't at all likely that he will grow more reliable with age!

"You will excuse me, won't you? I see Louise Smeed has just arrived and I have been trying to run her down for a week now."

Threading her arm through Demitria's, she tugged her off across the room to meet her friend, Louise.

"Encroaching old bitty!" she muttered under her breath as soon as they were out of earshot. "She is the worst sort of gossip, my dear, but never you mind. I gave her something to mull over!"

Glancing at Demi, she saw that Demi was looking both uncomfortable and frightened and patted her hand.

"Have faith, my dear. I am not without influence, and I have made it abundantly clear that you have my full support. They will not dare to snub you, whatever Horatia Wynthrope or Claudia Melbourne have to say."

Demi didn't feel particularly comforted, but there was little she could do in any case. Lady Wyndham refused to allow her to live quietly--'hide' as she put it. The first order of business once they reached town had been to visit all the local shops where, despite her protests, Lady Wyndham had ordered an enormous wardrobe for Demi--of the first stare of fashion, which was to say some of the gowns scandalized Demi. She simply could not bring herself to dampen her underskirts as Lady Wyndham did, which Lady Wyndham found highly amusing.

And well she might, Demi admitted privately, since she had not hesitated to behave completely scandalously with Lord Wyndham. On the other hand, that had been private ... to an extent, at least. Fortunately, she could only dimly recall the incident with Lord Wyndham on his horse, riding cross country where they might easily have been observed.

She hadn't been able to bring herself to mention that, however, ever hopeful that at least some of her transgressions would not come back to haunt her.

To Demi's great disappointment, Garrett not only did not arrive on their heels in town, he didn't arrive at all. Lady Wyndham kept her far too busy to spend much time moping over it, but she was not so occupied that she failed to notice his absence. She was deeply wounded over it. Obviously, both Sarah and Lady Wyndham had been wrong. He couldn't be desperately in love with her if she could be gone for weeks and weeks and he made no attempt to see her.

By the time they'd been in town for almost a month, Demi had begun to reconcile herself to the notion that he would not come because he not only didn't care, but because he was hoping she would find herself a husband and cease to be a thorn in his side. As dejected as she was, she decided that she should take Lady Wyndham's advice and consider whether she could find contentment with one of the young men who'd been courting her.

Naturally, none of the three she thought might possibly be serious in their intentions compared very favorably with Lord Wyndham. Mr. Collier was forever quoting poetry to her, and writing odes. She rather thought he fancied himself as a tortured poet, however, and not only was she fairly certain that she could not bear to listen endlessly to his attempts at poetry, but she began after a very little while to realize that he might actually prefer that she spurn him. That way he would be able to suffer endlessly over his 'lost love'. She also suspected that if she was to suddenly accept one of his frequent, passionate declarations of love that he would not quite know what to do about it. He was only a couple of years older than she was and he didn't quite strike her as a man about town who knew his way around a woman's boudoir.

Lord Thomas Melville was nearly as bad. He had no

interest in poetry, of course, for he fancied himself as a Corinthian--a sportsman of note. Unfortunately, he was rather unnervingly temperamental, and all too ready to issue, or accept, a challenge.

Lady Wyndham, to Demi's surprise, highly approved of him. Sighing, she would look at him and comment upon how lovely he was to the eye, and how much he reminded her of her late husband when he was a young man. Then she would add that Garrett had been much the same when he'd first come down from Oxford and that she'd despaired that he would live to see his thirtieth year, but he'd become quite adept with pistols and sword by the time he was five and twenty, and far less impulsive.

It was disconcerting to say the least. She couldn't decide whether Lady Wyndham was pointing out that Lord Melville would very likely make her a young widow, or that he would make a very good substitute for Garrett, being a great deal like him.

It was also disturbing to think that Garrett owed his continued good health to a prowess at dueling weapons and she couldn't help but have the uneasy feeling that there was a hint of a warning there that Garrett might call Lord Melville out, or vice versa if she was not careful.

In truth, she was far more tempted by the honorable, Sir Charles Curtis. He was a cheerful, very tolerant sort, and far more interested in hearth, home ... and hound, than London's social scene. Despite his penchant for hunting and shooting, however, he was a very good conversationalist and Demi always enjoyed his company. He was as fair as Garrett was dark, and of no more than medium height and build.

He was as different from Garrett as daylight to dark.

If it was not meant that she should be with Garrett, then she did not feel right about seeking anyone out only because he reminded her of Garrett. She didn't want to be reminded. She wanted to forget.

Sir Charles was no more or less than a country squire. Socially, he was beneath Lord Wyndham, which meant that even if they did wed and they did decide to socialize they would be in an entirely different social circle and unlikely to meet up.

To her surprise, when she expressed her opinion to Garrett's mother, Lady Wyndham did not approve. She said that Demi should not be so hasty to settle when she was perfectly willing, herself, to wait until she could introduce Demi more properly--to all of London society--the following season. They would close up her London residence and take a house in Bath for a few weeks and then, perhaps, they would join a few house parties in the country.

Only a few days before they were scheduled to leave for Bath, Garrett arrived in town at last.

* * * *

It had become Lady Wyndham's habit to come to Demi's room and help her to choose what she would wear on any given evening and direct the maids on how to pin her hair. Demi was not only perfectly willing to allow it, she was grateful to have someone who understood all of society's little idiosyncrasies well enough to direct her so that she didn't inadvertently dress in a manner that would draw ridicule or censure.

She had seemed rather distracted, however, to Demi's mind, directing the maid to try first one hair style and then another. Finally, after the third attempt, she had decided she was satisfied.

"Now for the perfect dress," she said. Getting to her feet, she moved to the armoire, discarding first one dress and then another and finally settling on the most beautiful, and most outrageous gown of the lot. The neckline was cut so low as to expose the upper edges of the pink aureoles of her nipples, while the fabric itself was shockingly sheer. Row upon row of tiny seed pearls had been sewn onto the fabric, creating flashes of color with each movement that riveted the eye, even if the shocking *décolleté* or the sheerness of the skirt failed to do so.

Demi looked it over doubtfully, but she did not object.

"Garrett has deigned to grace us with his presence," she said almost casually as the maid began to carefully work the gown over Demi's coiffure.

Demi's heart instantly leapt and began to race. "He is here?" she asked a little breathlessly.

Lady Wyndham shrugged irritably. "He was. I told him you were indisposed but that we would be at the Umphreys soiree later if he cared to join us."

"Oh," Demi said, immediately crestfallen.

Lady Wyndham gave her a look. "I will be severely put out with you, Demitria, if you are only going to behave like a complete ninny the moment you set eyes upon him."

Demi blushed. "I wouldn't."

"Yes, you would. If I have only to mention his name to have you all a flutter, I know very well that he will only have to crook an eyebrow at you to have you eating out of his hand and entirely willing to do anything that pleases him. It will *not* do!"

Demi studied Lady Wyndham thoughtfully, waiting until the maid had finished and departed, closing the door behind her. "What should I do then?"

Lady Wyndham smiled and patted the chair beside her. When Demi had seated herself, Lady Wyndham looked her over approvingly. "Garrett can be most charming when he wants something, Demi. He was fortunate enough to be born with both looks and money. Women have been throwing themselves at his head since he was scarcely out of leading strings. If you want him, you can not behave as all the others. You do want him?"

Demi debated briefly, but there seemed little point in denying it. She nodded.

"Then you can allow him only to come just so close and no closer. It certainly will not do to yield to him the moment he expresses a little interest. I know my son. He loves you. To my knowledge, he has never felt anything even approaching what he feels for you. However, he *is* a man, my dear. You must make him acknowledge it, both to himself, and to you. Until and unless he accepts the fact that he can not live without you, he will try to convince himself that he can. That will leave him in a position of complete power and you with none."

Demi frowned. "But I don't want power over him," she said hesitantly. "I just ... I want him to love me."

Lady Wyndham's brows rose. "Because?"

"Because?" Demi echoed.

Lady Wyndham rolled her eyes. "Why is it so important to you that he love you?"

"Why, because I love him."

"Exactly, and if you were to marry him and worship him, he would soon grow tired of being worshipped and look about for someone who was more of a challenge. The only way to catch a man and keep him--well anyone for that matter--is to make certain there is always the tiniest bit of doubt in the back of their mind that they have you completely."

Demi frowned. "It seems to me that would be difficult. In any case, I don't think he cares for me. If he did, wouldn't he have come before now?"

Lady Wyndham sighed. "*Life* is difficult, Demitria! Complacency is the road to ruin. And, as for that wretched son of mine--I confess I had not expected him to sulk quite so long in the country, but that is actually an advantage to us. It has given us time to establish you in society, and scotch those nasty rumors your aunt allowed to be fostered. Moreover, you now have your own beaus. A little competition never hurts."

Demi looked at Lady Wyndham uncomfortably. "You're not suggesting that I should encourage Sir Curtis, or Lord Melville only to make Garrett--Lord Wyndham jealous!"

Lady Wyndham studied her hands frowningly. "Of course not, my dear. But you are not planning to simply cut them out of your life, are you? That would be too cruel when you have encouraged them to believe you were interested."

"I hadn't thought of that!" Demi exclaimed in consternation. "I would not like to think that I'd ... wounded any of them."

Lady Wyndham waved her hand airily. "Posh! I know you would not purposefully wound anyone, Demi, but there are times when it can not be helped. You can not make up your mind whom you wish to select as your husband without allowing yourself to get to know them, and vice versa, and it is as inevitable as sunrise that someone's affections will be engaged, while another will remain impervious.

"That is the general way of things, you must know, my dear. It is rare indeed for two people to fall head over heels in love with each other. Most generally, they end up falling for someone who's in love with someone else and can not or will not return their regard.

"Now, we must be off. We want to be fashionably late, not rude."

Once they were settled in the carriage, Lady Wyndham fixed her with a stern eye. "You will take what I've said to heart?"

Demi sighed. "I do not think that I am very good at the art of flirtation, ma'am, but I do love Garrett and if this is what I must do, then I will do my best."

"Good!" Lady Wyndham said with a nod of approval. "It is perfectly acceptable to behave as if you are glad to see him, but you must not allow him to monopolize your time. That would be rude, in any case, and I know you wouldn't want to be thought rude."

Demi was far more nervous when they reached their destination even than she had been when she had attended her first social function with Lady Wyndham. She relaxed fractionally when she discovered that Lord Wyndham was not present, but she spent the first hour searching for him among the arriving guests. Finally, when he did not appear, depression set it, but even that did not last long.

Sir Charles Curtis and Mr. Lawrence Collier were in attendance and greeted her upon her arrival as if they had been waiting and watching for her. Sir Curtis immediately requested both her first dance and the supper dance. Mr. Collier, instead of retreating to a corner to assume a pose of great tragedy and adore her from a distance, secured the promise of the second dance.

Lord Melville, arriving upon the heels of her promises to the first two, examined her dance card, smiled wickedly at Sir Curtis and Mr. Collier and lay claim to her first waltz. Both Sir Curtis and Mr. Collier were immediately certain that they had been soundly trounced by the competition and neither made much attempt to hide their displeasure. As flattering as it was, it was also more than a little unsettling. She glanced around in search of Lady Wyndham, but to her relief, the musicians began to tune up for the first dance at that moment and she was able to remove both herself and Sir Curtis from the threatened unpleasantness.

By the time everyone began gravitating in the direction of the buffet, she'd managed to put Garrett from her mind, certain that he would not show after all, and she was able to actually enjoy both the company and the food.

The first strains of a waltz filtered through the gay chatter as they finished their meal and Demi glanced up to see Lord Melville threading his way through the crush to claim her. He quirked a dark eyebrow at her wickedly as their gazes met and she chuckled despite the fact that she knew very well he'd done it to provoke Sir Curtis, who'd looked around just as she had. As she looked away, her gaze locked with a pair of eyes that held absolutely no amusement, however.

Garrett was standing across the room speaking with several other guests. Her heart seemed to lurch against her chest wall and seize up, freezing the air in her lungs. It took an effort to disentangle her gaze from his and focus on Lord Melville as he presented himself at her table, and even more of an effort to smile in greeting. Something flickered in Lord Melville's eyes, and he glanced across the room as Demi had. She rose abruptly. "I'd wondered if you had forgotten me," she said a little breathlessly.

He turned to her then, his eyes alight with amusement and she realized with a touch of relief that he had not seen who had distracted her attention. If he'd caught the look Garrett was giving him, he would almost certainly have taken exception to it.

When they'd taken their positions in the dance, Demi breathed more easily. She'd more than half feared that Garrett might accost them before they reached the dance floor and there had been something distinctly unnerving about the look of repressed savagery in his features as he'd allowed his gaze to wander over her bodice and then studied both Sir Curtis and Lord Melville.

She'd never seen Garrett look quite that way. If that

was jealousy, she found it far more frightening than thrilling.

The strains of the waltz soothed her, however. She didn't think, despite the lessons Lady Wyndham had procured for her from the dance master, that she was more than adequate at the dance, but Lord Melville was both skilled and inherently graceful and more than made up for her own shortcomings. She relaxed as they glided across the floor, beginning to enjoy herself. The nervous flutter of her heart settled into the pleasurable rhythm of the dance.

Garrett met them at the edge of the dance floor. Bowing slightly, he dragged his gaze from Demi and looked Lord Melville over coolly. "Have I arrived too late to request the next waltz?" he asked pleasantly.

"No," Demi said a little breathlessly.

"As a matter of fact ... yes," Lord Melville responded at almost the same moment. "I am before you, Wyndham."

Garrett's eyes hardened. The half smile on his lips never wavered, however. "I believe you are mistaken, Melville."

Demi felt the blood leave her face as she glanced from one man to the other. Forcing a tight smile, she gripped her dance card in a white knuckled fist. "Actually, I had promised--" she began.

"Garrett! I'm so glad to see that you have made it after all," Lady Wyndham interrupted as she joined them. "I suppose I should not be surprised to discover the two most handsome and dashing men in the room hovered about my ward, but I am most put out with the two of you. Especially you, Thomas! Naughty boy! I suppose you will tell me it has slipped your mind that you promised me a waltz?"

Something flickered in his eyes, but he smiled at her engagingly. "I would never forget a promise made to such a beautiful woman," he murmured with a slight bow.

Lady Wyndham swatted his arm with her fan. "Flatterer! I know very well that you only see me as an old woman, but it is very sweet of you nevertheless."

Chuckling, he offered his arm to her. "If you will

excuse us?"

Demi looked at Garrett nervously when the two had left but took his arm when he offered it. "Will you join me for dinner?"

Demi glanced at him uneasily. "I have already been downstairs to eat."

"Which does not necessarily preclude your joining me."

Demi frowned. "I had promised the next dance to Mr. Collier. I would be very rude to break my promise."

Garrett shrugged. "The musicians are taking a break. I will have you back before they strike up once more."

She sighed uneasily but nodded. Lady Wyndham had told her under no circumstances to allow Garrett to get her alone, but there were bound to be others lingering downstairs over a late supper. They met no one as they descended the stairs, however, and uneasiness swept over Demi once more.

"I must suppose my mother commissioned that gown," Garrett said pensively.

Demi glanced at him sharply. "She said the ones I had were far too dowdy."

"Certainly by comparison," he said coolly, pausing at the foot of the stairs and turning to look her over. Taking her hand once more, he held it as she stepped down the remaining stairs, then tucked it into the crook of his arm once more as he led her down the corridor toward the dining room. "And I've no doubt at all that it is vastly appreciated, for I saw no less than a half a dozen young bucks eyeing you lasciviously as you danced with Lord Melville. Is there any particular reason that you are encouraging them to hang after you, I wonder?"

Demi gaped at him indignantly. "Exactly what is it that you are accusing me of?" she demanded, jerking her hand free and stopping abruptly to glare at him.

He caught her shoulders, pushing her back against the wall and pinning her there. "Being too available?" he suggested. "Why has our engagement not been announced? I gave my mother specific instructions to do so."

Demi blushed, but realized at his second question that

she'd misunderstood the first comment. She thought she had, at any rate. "Because I have not received a proposal?" she said sharply. "Perhaps you should ask your mother since it was her you spoke to?"

He studied her a long moment. "You can not have doubted my intentions."

Hurt abruptly replaced her anger. She swallowed with some difficulty. "I didn't, until I discovered you had taken me to your mother. Then I realized it was a matter of honor and a misplaced sense of obligation. Lady Wyndham has assured me it's unnecessary for you to make such a ... sacrifice on my account."

He ground his teeth. "Did she?"

"Yes. She also said that she would be happy to be my guardian until I was settled."

"And Lord Melville, I take it, now ranks among your many beaus?"

Demi flushed, detecting a hint of sarcasm as well as censure. "You would have to ask him what his intentions are. He has not asked for me, if that is what you mean."

"Oh, I will ask him. Make no doubt of that."

Demi felt the blood rush from her face. "What do you mean by that?"

"Do I detect concern for young Melville's hide?" he ground out.

Her eyes widened. "Garrett! You wouldn't!"

"You are mine, Demi. Make no mistake--I would."

She flushed. "Only because you ... we--"

"Exactly because I, we," he growled. Reaching up, he very deliberately scooped one breast from the demi cup of her gown, covering it with the heat of his mouth. Sensation exploded inside of her at the moist adhesion of his mouth that seemed to pull every ounce of will from her, wrenching the strength from her knees. Dizzy with the pleasure coursing through her, she looked around the empty corridor with a vague sense of alarm, knowing someone might come upon them at any moment.

"Garrett! Please!"

He released her breast, fondling it with his hand as he met her gaze. His breath, sawing raggedly in and out of his chest, sent a shiver through her as it brushed her damp, distended nipple. "It pleases me a great deal to please you." He brushed his lips lightly across hers. Briefly, he covered her mouth, kissing her with devastating thoroughness before he released her lips. "You are mine. You want me as much as I want you. I can convince you of it very easily."

Demi swallowed, her mind so fogged with desire she could scarcely make any sense of what he was demanding of her. She could not think of anything beyond the fact that she wanted him never to stop, and she feared being disgraced if someone happened upon them. It wasn't until he dipped his head and took her breast into his mouth once more that she realized that he was demanding an answer from her, but the moment he began kissing her once more, her wits scattered into the fog of desire. She could not jog her mind past the deliciously wicked pleasure coursing through her, the clenching and unclenching of the muscles low in her belly in precise rhythm to the ministrations of his mouth and tongue.

The sound of voices filtered slowly through her heated brain and the scrape of footsteps on the stairs jolted through her. She moistened her lips. "Yes," she whispered a little desperately. He released her at once, tucking her breast into her bodice once more.

In a heated confusion, she watched as he adjusted himself. It dissipated abruptly as her gaze focused on the telltale ridge of flesh that bulged against the front of his trousers from his waistband downward.

Such a display of manly flesh could hardly go unnoticed. Glancing down, she noticed her flesh above her bodice was reddened from the abrasion of his whiskers. From the faint tingling around her mouth, she had not doubt she looked as thoroughly kissed, as well.

Chapter Seventeen

"Here you are, my dear!" Lady Wyndham said gaily as she reached the bottom on the stairs. "The supper room was closed nigh an hour ago!"

"So we discovered," Garrett said easily, although his voice was still husky and deep.

Lady Wyndham's gaze flickered over them, but it was impossible to tell from her expression what must be going through her mind. Demi only hoped that the corridor was not so bright that she could discern immediately what she'd interrupted. "I have offered to give Lady Shelley a ride home, my dear. I hope you won't mind leaving a little early?"

"I will give her a ride home, mother," Garrett said at once.

Demi flicked a glance from Garrett to his mother and managed a faint smile. "I do appreciate it, my lord, but I have a touch of headache. I believe I will go with Lady Wyndham."

He studied her a long moment and finally bowed, saluting her hand. "Until tomorrow then."

She was relieved when they settled in Lady Wyndham's coach, but worried that either Lady Wyndham or worse, Lady Shelley, might have noticed something in her behavior. Either Lady Shelley was a very good actress, however, or she'd had too much on her mind to notice. She could talk of nothing all the way home but her anxiety over her young daughter's illness, which was why she'd been summoned home.

When they'd set her down, Demi fully expected a thorough dressing down. Lady Wyndham surprised her by smiling. "You did very well, my dear."

"I did?" Demi said in surprise.

Lady Wyndham chuckled. "Naughty! But it will not hurt to allow Garrett a taste of what he will miss if he does not play his cards right."

Demi blushed to the roots of her hair. "But he only

...it was only a kiss."

Her brows rose. "I should think it was a bit more than that. I must say I hadn't realize my son was such a strapping young man. No wonder--never mind. It will do him no harm to suffer a little. I believe we will leave for Bath in the morning," she added pensively.

"Tomorrow? But he has only just arrived in town," Demi objected.

"Mmm and on the hunt, make no doubt, but I'm of no mind to make things easy for him. We will most certainly leave for Bath. I will reserve judgment until I've seen how long it takes him to take the scent. If he's to go off and sulk each time you slip through his fingers it will certainly serve him right if another man snaps you up."

Demi studied Lady Wyndham uncomfortably. "What if he gives up?"

"Then he doesn't deserve you, my dear. He's had months to pop the question and instead he has dillied about like a green boy instead of approaching you straight away and making certain he fixed your attentions. I confess, I find this as intriguing as it is frustrating. It can only mean he is completely besotted with you, whatever you think of it. He would not be so anxious, or clumsy, if it did not mean a great deal to him. Take my word for it, he has never been shy before."

Demi grimaced wryly. She wouldn't call him shy precisely. She was rather more inclined to think his intentions had never been honorable and that he'd approached her exactly as he'd meant to, clandestinely, because he'd never meant to offer her anything more than a slip on the shoulder.

"I see the wheels of your mind turning, but you will allow that I am vastly more experienced than you, my dear, and I know my son. He told me months ago that he had decided that it was time to settle down and that he had his eye on someone."

Demi twisted her hands in her lap. "But he didn't say it was me."

Lady Wyndham waved that away. "He didn't need to. It was as plain as the nose on your face. It is just as

Sarah said. From the moment you entered any room, he rarely took his eyes from you."

Demi said nothing, for she was certain she would have noticed herself if that had been the case. The mention of Sarah distracted her, however. "I thought Sarah was to be my maid."

Lady Wyndham shrugged. "I left her in the country for further training. In any case, she has already proven that she can be trusted to allow you to wrap her around your finger at any time you want something, whether it is good for you or not. You are putty in my son's hands and need someone about you to shake a bit of sense into you … not someone who is putty in *your* hands."

Demi flushed, but she could hardly deny the accusations.

She was relieved when they reached Lady Wyndham's townhouse. The head ache she'd claimed had manifested itself and she excused herself and went directly up to her room. She'd only just settled in her bed when she heard the commotion downstairs of an arrival. Her heart immediately leapt as it occurred to her that it might be Garrett, but she knew Lady Wyndham would be extremely displeased with her if she leapt from the bed and dressed herself once more.

In a little while, the guest departed once more. Shortly afterwards, Lady Wyndham arrived at her door, tapped lightly and entered, a devilish smile curling her lips.

"Who was it?"

Lady Wyndham chuckled. "My son, of course. I had the butler tell him that we had retired for the evening and that he should call around tomorrow at a decent hour."

Demi's eyes widened. "I thought we were leaving in the morning?"

"We are, my dear. Garrett will almost certainly be most put out."

Demi was dismayed, but despite that, Lady Wyndham was so obviously enjoying herself hugely that she couldn't help but be amused as well.

"You are not worried that he will be furious with us both?"

She laughed. "I'm counting on it!"

Demi was exhausted by the time they arrived in Bath, both physically and emotionally. She might have been inclined to think the grueling pace they set was in the nature of flight except for the fact that they had set a similar pace when they had left Wyndham Park for London and it had become clear that Lady Wyndham was not one who cared to travel sedately. She focused completely upon her destination and wanted no time wasted in reaching it.

Despite that, the coach was no match for a determined rider. Sir Curtis and Lord Melville set out with them as escorts. Garrett and Mr. Collier caught up with them on the road.

One look at the set of Garrett's jaw was enough to assure both ladies that he wasn't at all pleased with the turn of events. Since Lady Wyndham had had the forethought to have the servants pack a basket for them, however, he was not given the opportunity to express his displeasure before they reached Bath.

When they reached Bath, Lady Wyndham thanked their escorts and dismissed them, assuring them that they would be at home to visitors the following day. Garrett refused to take the hint and followed them inside.

"I must suppose my memory is at fault, for I do not recall that you said that you would be leaving London for Bath today," he said tightly the moment the door closed behind them.

Lady Wyndham lifted her brows at him, but instead of commenting immediately, she turned to Demi. "You must run up to your room and rest, my dear. I can see you are quite pale with fatigue."

She nodded wordlessly. The truth was she was tired, but she was also anxious to escape the confrontation she could see brewing between Lady Wyndham and her son. Garrett stopped her, caressing her cheek lightly and she looked up at him with a mixture of surprise and doubt. His expression was more worried than angry, however. "You are certain you are not taking ill?"

Demi shook her head. "I am only tired."

He released her, but she felt his gaze on her back as she climbed the stairs.

"I was certain I must have told you we would be removing to Bath," Lady Wyndham said airily, drawing his attention as she turned and made her way into the parlor. She inspected it cursorily to make certain the servants she'd sent down the night before had cleaned it thoroughly and finally settled on the settee. "It was growing far too hot to remain in London and we had made the plans more than a week ago."

Garrett's lips tightened. "I only just arrived in London," he said coolly.

Her brows rose. "Well, I must suppose that is why you hadn't heard," she retorted. "I'd expected you to follow us weeks ago."

His eyes narrowed, instead of answering her at once, however, he paced to the window and stood looking out, his back to the room. "I had business that needed attending at Wyndham Park that had been neglected in my absence."

Lady Wyndham released an irritated sigh. She didn't doubt that it was true, but she did not believe the business of the estate could have required so much of his time. "Well, we are here now."

"For how long?"

She shrugged, although she knew he was still facing the street and couldn't see her. "Until we are ready to move on ... a few weeks, certainly."

"What game is this the two of you are playing at?" he asked, his voice deceptively soft.

Lady Wyndham uttered an irritated hiss of displeasure. "I should ask the same of you."

He turned to study her for several moments. "Then I will tell you 'tis no game I play. I am in deadly earnest, mother."

She might have been tempted to dismiss the remark except there was something in his demeanor that she had not seen before. She rather thought his opponents on the dueling field might have, but she had not. Uneasiness touched her, but not altogether because she saw very clearly that he was, indeed, deadly serious.

She was almost certain that Demi was with child. Demi did not seem to be aware of it yet, and she was fairly certain that Garrett did not suspect, or hadn't until a few moments ago when he had studied her so searchingly.

She had undertaken to teach Garrett a lesson, not only because she felt he was in dire need of it, given his most ungentlemanly behavior, but also because she loved him. She did not want to see him hurt by his own hardheaded determination to refuse to acknowledge his feelings for Demi--or Demitria either, for that matter. It was all very well to speak of complacency, but if Garrett could convince himself that it was not so, then he might also convince himself that he had wed her only because he was duty bound to do so after he'd dishonored her, and that way led to disaster.

On the other hand, if it was true that Demi was with child, she was playing with fire and they might all be burned.

"Demi is not playing any game at all. She simply could not bear to think that she was an object of misplaced duty. I told her she did not need to settle for so little. She is a sweet girl. I love her quite as much, I think, as if she had been my own daughter. She deserves a man who loves her. Hopefully one whom she holds in high regard, as well. I have every confidence that she will receive a proposal from Sir Curtis, and very likely Lord Melville, as well, before the summer is out."

"She is *mine!*" he ground out furiously. "I will not allow you to interfere, mother!"

Lady Wyndham was more than a little discomposed by the underlying fury in his voice, but she wasn't about to allow him to think he could cow her merely by roaring at her. She gave him a look. "You are not a savage, Garrett! You are a lord of the realm! You can not simply throw her to the dirt and claim her as if you are some conquering barbarian!

"I can not say that she has behaved just as she ought, but she is a lady, nevertheless, and neither can I, of all people, sit in judgment."

Garrett studied her in silence for several moments. "It is not your place to interfere in my life either, mother, especially when you know very well that my sense of obligation is warranted and that that is only a part of it."

Lady Wyndham looked at him in despair. "I know nothing beyond the fact that you have behaved abominably toward that girl! And neither does she, for that matter."

He flushed, but he didn't dispute it. Lady Wyndham studied him for several moments and finally decided that she had kept her own council long enough. If there was any chance that speaking would help Garrett to understand, then she owed it to him to tell him the truth. She sighed, feeling a welling of sick fear, but whether Garrett hated her once she'd told him or not, she loved him enough that she felt that it was worth it.

"I don't know how much you remember about your father. I've never spoken of him to you ... not really."

Garrett sent her a frowning glance of confusion. "I'm afraid I can not see the relevance of telling me at this late date," he said tightly.

"I'm telling you now precisely because it *is* relevant," his mother snapped. "I should have told you long ago, but I was such a coward. And, truth be told, I figured sooner or later you would learn of it anyway, for there's no getting around the fact that it was a scandal."

A faint smile curled his lips. "I am well aware that you are no saint, mother."

She blushed faintly but shook her head. "I was mad for your father. Sometimes, looking back, I think I truly wasn't entirely sane. I worshipped him almost from the first moment we met. I would have done anything for him. I was perfectly willing to do anything he asked of me ... eager actually. Which is why it is so easy for me to understand Demi.

"What happened next was almost inevitable. I found that I was with child. It frightened me so badly I could think of nothing but telling your father and he, naturally, assured me he would do right by me, which he did.

"He was still quite young, however. We both were, but I think he resented me for forcing him into responsibility before he was ready for it. I always believed he did. Eventually, I began to see that my love for him was only hurting me. He never told me he loved me. He allowed me to believe that he had only wed me because he knew he was honor bound to do so. Maybe that was all he ever felt. I never knew, but I did finally realize that I could not go on wondering, doubting.

"I set out to kill my affection for him. It was the only way that I felt that I could find peace. I don't suppose I ever did stop loving him, but in the end, it didn't matter."

Her chin wobbled slightly as she looked up at him. "It was my fault he was killed ... the duel ... it was because of me. I don't expect you to excuse me, or forgive me. I never could forgive myself."

Garrett sat heavily in the chair facing the settee where she sat, as if his knees had given out. "He believed you had been unfaithful."

Lady Wyndham nodded. There were tears streaming down her cheeks now, but she made no effort to brush them away. "I don't expect you to believe me, but I wasn't. I still loved him, in spite of everything, but he seemed to want me to go my own way. He had his own interests, and they rarely, if ever, included me. I thought that he would be more content if I accepted the way things were and I suppose I hoped that he would want me if I wasn't quite so ... desperate to please.

"It was not at all uncommon for married women to have young attached males escort them. It never occurred to me that he would fly into such a rage over it, that he would assume things happened that had not." She shook her head. "You see, I am still trying to make excuses for myself, trying to understand, trying to live with what happened. And I have had this awful fear that history was about to repeat itself.

"If you do not care for her, even just a little, Garrett, be kind and let her go. You have both made one terrible mistake already. Do not pay for it in blood. I will take care of Demi. The right man will love her in spite of what has happened and forgive her for being human and less than perfect."

Garrett studied her for several moments and finally scrubbed his hands over his face, rubbing his eyes tiredly. When he looked up at her again, he swallowed convulsively before he spoke. "I think...." He paused and smiled crookedly. "I think I am my mother's son. I love her, mother. So much it scares the hell out of me."

He stood abruptly and began pacing. "I have made the most damnable mess of things. What am I to do?"

Lady Wyndham didn't know whether to laugh or cry. She did a little of both. "Tell her, you fool! You can not surely doubt that she adores you every bit as much, if not more?"

Garrett's gaze went at once to the ceiling, as if he could see through it and into Demi's room. He swallowed convulsively, turning a slightly sickly color. "Now?" he said doubtfully.

Lady Wyndham gave him a look. "For God's sake, Garrett! The child will be grown before you gather your nerve at this rate!"

Chapter Eighteen

"Child?" Garrett echoed blankly. He transformed before her eyes into a raging barbarian once more. "Mother!"

"Don't use that tone with me, Garrett! I'm still your mother. As it happens, I'm not entirely certain of it myself, and I don't think Demi's figured it out either. Nevertheless...."

Garrett slammed the door so hard on his way out, the windows rattled. Lady Wyndham bit her lip as she heard him taking the stairs two at the time. Finally, she shrugged. It was long past time they handled their own affairs. She felt certain that Garrett would figure it out.

An odd sort of peace settled over her. Garrett had always been the very image of his father. It had been a source of both pleasure and pain for her, and now she thought it had given her a measure of peace, as well. She thought, perhaps, that Gerard truly had loved her in his own way, in spite of the circumstances surrounding their marriage. Perhaps, like Garrett, he had simply found that it was something too difficult to express, a weakness he was fearful of disclosing?

* * * *

Demi was half asleep when the door burst open abruptly. It jolted her wide awake, however, and she sat and stared at the furious man at her door in consternation. Garrett surveyed the room, his eyes narrowing on the startled maid by the window.

"*Out!*"

The woman gaped at him. "My lord?"

"*Out!*"

Sending a frightened glance at Demi, she bolted for the door. He closed it firmly behind her and locked it. Demi swallowed uneasily. "Garrett?" she gasped a little doubtfully.

Her eyes widened as he shrugged out of his jacket and dropped it to the floor, then tugged his cravat loose and tossed that aside, as well. "Are you mad! Lady Wyndham--the servants!"

He shrugged, popping the buttons from his vest as he tore it open impatiently instead of unbuttoning it. Leaning down, he tugged first one boot off and then the other, dropping them to the floor with a clatter. "Yes."

Demi blinked, dragging her gaze from the evidence of his arousal with an effort. "What?"

"I believe there is a very good chance that I am mad. I have published the banns, but I do not believe I have the patience to wait until we have said our vows. In fact, I'm certain of it."

She held out her hand as if to stop him. "Garrett, this isn't--you shouldn't have done that. It wasn't necessary."

"Unfortunately, it was. It is required and I could not find a way around it, beyond making a mad dash for Greta Green--which I have no intention of doing." The shirt joined the pile of clothing near the door. Demi covered her eyes as he shucked his breeches and linens.

"But-but Garrett, I don't want you to feel that you have to marry me!"

She felt the bed shift as he settled on it beside her. His hands closed over her wrists, pulling her hands away from her eyes. She looked at him wide-eyed, unnerved by the glitter in his eyes as much as she was by the tense set of his expression.

"You can not save me from my folly, Demi. God's truth, I don't think I could bear it if you tried." Lifting a hand, he stroked her cheek gently. "If you feel you can not love me, Demi, I will learn to live with it, but I'm fairly certain I can not learn to live without you. I know I don't want to."

Tears filled her eyes and clogged her throat so that she couldn't speak for several moments. "How could you possibly believe that I didn't love you? You must know that I do."

Slipping his hand from her cheek to the back of her head, he leaned toward her and kissed her, his lips moving over hers in a gentle caress, fitting, molding and then separating from hers in tiny kisses that were almost tentative, as if he were uncertain, still, of his reception.

Demi slipped one arm around his shoulder and the other around his waist, surrendering without protest. He deepened the kiss, covering her mouth with his own and plunging his tongue inside to taste and touch and explore the sensitive inner surfaces possessively. She kissed him back almost with a sense of desperation as need, long denied, surfaced, began to overwhelm her.

Disappointment flooded her as he pulled away. He placed a finger to her lips, traced them, and then traced a trail downward. With fingers that shook noticeably, he loosened the tie at the neck of her gown and tugged it off, tossing it across the room to join his own clothing. He pushed her back among the pillows then, pushing the covers away and studying her body in a leisurely way that made heat and tension curl inside of her.

She shifted uncertainly and he placed his palm on her shoulder, skating it down her arm lightly. Moving over her, he stroked and kissed her slowly, almost methodically, from her shoulders all the way to her toes, missing nothing, leaving no part of her unexplored. Demi was writhing feverishly beneath his caresses, moaning almost incessantly long before he reached her feet and dizzy with need. Kneeling at the foot of the bed, he caught her ankles and pushed them up the bed until her knees were bent, her legs spread wantonly.

Looking down at him she saw that he was studying her woman's flesh, his gaze liquid with fire, his face taut with hunger. As if he felt her gaze, he looked up at her. Holding her gaze, he leaned toward her slowly and opened his mouth, kissing her there as he had her breasts, with the moist adhesion of his mouth, the teasing torment of his tongue. Demi gasped at the intense pleasure that ripped through her, reaching for him blindly. He caught her wrists, closing her hands over her ankles and holding them there as he continued to tease and suckle the tiny bud above her femininity until, abruptly, shock waves of pleasure exploded through her and she cried out.

Grasping her hips, he shifted onto his knees and sheathed his flesh deeply within hers while the muscles in her passage continued to quake in shattering release. Slipping hands beneath her, he pulled her upright, so that she was straddling him as she had that day on horseback, riding him. She wrapped her arms tightly around his shoulders, allowing her mind to recapture those moments, feeling the same rush of excitement flood her as she moved in rapid counterpoint to each thrust.

Within moments, she felt her body racing with his toward completion and when his arms tightened around her and he groaned his release, her body convulsed in a mind shattering climax. His arms tightened around her as she felt her body go limp with release. Almost reluctantly, he lowered her back onto the pillows and moved away from her. Settling beside her, he stroked her soothingly.

"Your mother will be wroth with us," she said finally when she had caught her breath. "She has been at such pains to make me respectable."

Chuckling, Garrett pushed himself up until he was propped against the headboard and dragged her across his lap, stroking her hair back from her face and soothing it with his hands. "I think she has achieved precisely what she intended ... perhaps not exactly as she had intended, but she is not one to quibble over the details."

Demi looked at him a little uncertainly, but he only shook his head, smiling faintly as he settled his hand over her belly, cupping it, stroking it. Demi stared down at his hand, feeling the heat of it sink into her. Slowly, as she glanced from the expression on his face to his hand, understanding dawned. "You knew!" she gasped.

His gaze flew to hers and lingered for several heartbeats before it returned to his hand. The half smile became a satisfied grin. "I do now."

"That wasn't--it's not because you thought I was with child?"

He studied her seriously for a long moment. "The first time I ever saw you, you took my breath."

Happiness and doubt washed through her in equal measure. "Truly?"

"Absolutely."

"When?"

His lips twisted. "I can not recall."

She frowned. "Well, what was I wearing?"

He frowned thoughtfully and finally smiled. "The most beautiful smile I have even seen. But I think it was the look in your eyes that stopped my heart."

Demi blushed. "What look?" she asked uneasily.

"I'm not at all certain … love, I think. I saw a woman who looked at me as if I was the most wonderful man in the world, and it made me feel as if I was, or at least as if I wanted to be as wonderful as you thought."

Uncomfortable, she traced the pattern of hair on his chest. "Maybe." She looked up at him again. "Probably."

"The one thing I am absolutely certain of is that I could think of nothing else … nor gather the nerve to approach you. At first, I think it was because I was afraid that I'd see that light in your eyes dim if you saw me for who I really was. Later it was that dragon aunt of yours. By that time, she'd decided that it was Phoebe I was interested in. I didn't know what she might do to you if she realized I only had eyes for you."

He cupped her face in his hands and leaned down to kiss her lightly on the lips. "There are many very good reasons why I should marry you, Demi, but don't for one moment believe that any of it is even half as important as the fact that I love you."

The End

Printed in the United States
38951LVS00003B/4-162